THE
MONSTERS' ROOM

THE MONSTERS' ROOM

(original title: Peter's Angel)

by Hope Campbell

illustrated by Lilian Obligado

SCHOLASTIC BOOK SERVICES
NEW YORK · TORONTO · LONDON · AUCKLAND · SYDNEY · TOKYO

ISBN 0-590-02076-5

A hardcover edition of this book is published by Four Winds Press, a division of Scholastic, under the title PETER'S ANGEL, and is available through your local bookstore or directly from Four Winds Press, 730 Broadway, New York, NY 10003.

12 11 10 9 8 7 6   2 3 4 5 6/8

For John
and
all his friends

1

For the first time since they had come to live with him, Peter had forgotten to feed his mice. The worst thing about it was that he didn't remember he had forgotten. His mind was taken up with other matters.

As he walked to school with his best friend Obie one autumn morning. Peter was thinking about monsters. He had a serious problem. He didn't know how to tell Obie something very important.

He could say, "Obie, I think the monsters are getting out of hand."

He could say, "Obie, I hate to tell you this, but those monsters have become entirely mine, not yours."

No, that might hurt Obie's feelings too much.

He could say, "Obie, maybe we'd better stop the Club."

Obie would never understand.

He could say, "Obie, you may find this hard to believe, but those monsters are *real*."

Obie would think Peter was losing his mind.

Of course, he could tell the truth—he could say, "Hey, Obie, I'm getting scared!"

Would his best friend think he was a coward? Just a weak, faint-hearted, lily-livered chicken-sissy? (One of Obie's favorite phrases.) Peter couldn't imagine anything worse. He gave a loud sigh. He couldn't think of any way to say it.

While Peter lagged behind, Obie trotted ahead swinging his briefcase. His real name was Osbert Macbeth Macduff and he hated all three of his names.

"They're what you call German shepherds or greyhounds," Obie would say. "People name big dogs Macbeth and Macduff. Even Osbert," he would add gloomily, "sounds like a name for a beagle."

Peter was simply Peter James Wood, and Obie was always complaining enviously, "I wish I had a short, neat name like yours."

Peter and Obie lived in the same apartment house in the city, they went to the same school, and together they had the best Monster Club in town. The headquarters were in Peter's room because his parents allowed it. Obie's parents refused to have any monsters about.

There was one other member of the club, and to tell the truth, they hadn't wanted her in it at all. But Sally Elaine Lorrimor had a way of getting into things. She went to a different school, but lived in the same building, on the sixteenth floor. Like Obie, she hated her name.

She said Sally Elaine Lorrimor sounded like "worms sliding around after a storm." Since she prided herself on being tough, and planned to be a brain surgeon when she grew up, she wouldn't let anyone call her Sally.

"Did you ever hear of a brain surgeon named Sally? No, I have to be 'Sal' because it doesn't sound like worms and it's a nice, in-between name. Nobody will know who I am, boy, girl, or thing."

When Peter and Osbert and Sally were together, they liked being plain Pete, Obie, and Sal.

Most of the time Peter and Obie used their student passes to take the Broadway bus. But on fine mornings they liked to walk up the tree-lined sidewalk on Riverside Drive. They had to wear suits and ties to their school (which was private and Episcopalian), and when they walked they could undo their ties, unbutton their collars, open their jackets, and unzip their winter coats. Then they would run wild, letting the cold air and wind hit their chests.

Their mothers hated the whole idea. They were afraid the boys would catch cold, which Peter and Obie wouldn't have minded a bit. They loved staying home sick. Particularly in the Monster Club.

Obie ran ahead and jumped at a branch. He was nine, like Peter, but a little shorter and fatter. Peter had always thought Obie looked a bit like a baby walrus. Watching him jump made Peter jealous. Obie always had such energy in the morning! As usual Peter was exhausted after a night with the monsters.

"Hey, Pete," called Obie. "The new magazine comes out today. It's got a terrific spread on *Creature from the Black Lagoon.*"

Peter shuddered. He knew quite enough about that creature already.

"And I think there's a new one, from a brand new movie," said Obie. "Mighty Mud Monster or something."

Oh, no! Peter already had the Mud Men Twins, and he was sick of them gurgling and slurping and dripping around the house. If there were any new monsters in the monthly horror magazine, they might decide to come live with him too, in his already crowded room!

4

"We don't have to get the new magazine, do we?" he asked Obie. "Don't we have enough magazines already?"

"Enough!" yelled Obie. "We only have seventy-six!"

Peter heard a few hoots from behind the trees. He jumped and looked over his shoulder. Not one monster to be seen! But they loved to trick him like that, to hide behind tree trunks and hoot and call and sometimes jump out to startle him.

"I ... I don't have enough money for the magazine," lied Peter.

"What about your lunch money?" cried Obie, astonished. "Did you forget it?"

It was sad but true that all the monster magazines and horror comics, the pictures, masks, bugs, and models came directly out of Peter's lunch money.

Mrs. Wood had made a mistake. She had not paid the school in advance for hot lunch. Obie's mother had. So Obie never had any extra change. But every day Peter's mother gave him the exact amount for a hot, nourishing, midday meal, and every day Peter bought a cheap cold sandwich instead.

He and Obie squandered the rest of the money on monsters. Each day when he walked in with a new comic book or rubber creature, Peter would say to his mother, "Oh, this? Obie bought it for me."

Mrs. Wood thought that Obie's parents gave him far too much allowance, but she couln't complain because Obie seemed "such a generous boy."

For the first time the idea made Peter angry. "The money I've spent on that Horde!" he thought. "And not one of them deserves it."

It made him so angry that he was short with Obie. He even lied again. "I brought the money but I have to use it. i didn't have any breakfast."

No breakfast was the lie. Peter's mother believed in nourishing breakfasts as much as she believed in hot lunches. Every morning she stuffed Peter with grapefruit, natural cereal with wheat germ, fortified milk, and vitamins.

Nobody needed a hot lunch after a breakfast like that went Peter's excuse for lying to his mother. He was used to lying to her, but not to Obie. It felt strange.

"No breakfast!" said Obie. "What happened?"

"Mother...uh...Mother was sick," lied Peter for the third time.

In back of him there was sudden loud laughter and applause. Peter winced. Obie, of course, hadn't heard a thing. He never did.

"What'll we do?" cried Obie. "We always get the magazine on the first day."

6

"I don't really feel like it today," said Peter slowly.

He trudged ahead, kicking up piles of autumn leaves from the sidewalk. It was November and the trees above were beginning to look bare.

"You know, you're acting funny," observed Obie. "And you look funny too."

"Do I?"

"Yes. You don't seem so interested in the Club anymore. You act weird. And your eyes are all hollow."

Peter knew. He'd seen himself in the mirror. He was very white and thin, his hair hung in limp points, and he even had circles under his eyes. He had a secret fear that he looked a little like a monster himself.

"Maybe...maybe it's too many monsters," he started to say.

But Obie interrupted, "Maybe you *should* have a hot lunch. Say! Why don't you eat mine, and I'll have a cold sandwich, and then we can still use your money!"

Foiled! Peter couldn't object to Obie's plan because it was so logical.

They reached the cross street for the school and waited for the light to change. Peter held Obie's briefcase while Obie tied his tie and buttoned his collar and jacket. Then Obie did the same for

7

Peter. When the light changed they ran across the street and then walked slowly to the school door.

"Another boring day!" proclaimed Obie dramatically. "Oh, well. I'll meet you here, right after school."

He stuck out his hand, palm down.

Reluctantly, Peter slid his hand under Obie's. He didn't really want to do this anymore, but they'd whispered the Secret Oath to each other every day for a year, as loyal monster fans.

Monsters many and monsters mighty,
Monsters forever, day and nightly!

Obie slapped Peter's palm. "See you."

He went inside—they were in different classes—and Peter glanced back at the sidewalk.

Of course! The moment Obie was gone *they* decided to come out of hiding. They were lined up halfway down the street, leaning on lamp posts and parked cars. The Mud Men lifted their thick, oozing arms in greeting. Wolf Demon grinned and wiggled his pointed ears. Blue Blob and Yellow Slime started flowing toward the school steps. Frankie (Peter's nickname for Dr. Frankenstein's nameless monster) waved his huge, gloved hands like an orchestra conductor, trying to keep order.

"Hold on boys," Peter heard him say. "We can't go in yet. Calm down and control yourselves."

They were always furious if Peter didn't wave at them. They'd be even more disruptive in class and later on, at home. So Peter smiled at the Horde—it was a rather weak smile—and made a small motion with his hands that he hoped none of the other kids would see. Then he turned and went into school.

Now! He took a deep, relieved breath. He would have thirty minutes of peace. Thirty whole minutes without the monsters — in morning Chapel.

The boys and girls were halfway through their prayer when Peter remembered something. "Forgive us our trespasses," all the children were saying. Peter became silent. The boy sitting next to him jogged his elbow, but Peter couldn't utter another word.

He had forgotten something for the first time. He had forgotten to leave out food for his mice. His friends, his little creatures, the only creatures he had except monsters! He felt like a father to them. They were completely dependent on him. And he had forgotten.

He stared blankly at the large picture of the angel behind the altar, and two huge tears slowly rolled down his cheeks.

The Sister who taught his class was sitting in the

same row. She noticed, and thought he was having a religious experience. She hoped it was an attack of conscience and that he'd do better in class to-day.

But Peter was thinking, "I *must* be losing my mind! Those monsters are ruining me. I'm tired and weak and pale. I cry too easily, I get no sleep, I'm forgetting very important things — and I'm not doing anything about it!

"I wonder if I am just a miserable coward after all?"

2

While Peter was at school, the mice ventured forth from their home behind the walls, into Peter's room. Of course they weren't "his" mice at all. Their names were Mr. and Mrs. Eben and Eliza Starbuck and they were perfectly independent, older mice with grown children and grandchildren of their own. Eliza had soft gray fur and Eben's whiskers were turning white.

Like any grown-up persons would, they shook their heads at Peter's collection of horrors.

"It gets worse and worse," said Eliza. Her whiskers quivered with disapproval.

"Yes, it really is quite, um, monstrous," said Eben deliberately.

Not an inch of Peter's walls was without a monster picture. There were small pictures, medium-sized ones, magazine covers, and several life-sized movie posters. The bookcases were filled with monster magazines and horror comics. The toy shelves didn't hold toys anymore; they displayed rows of plastic monster figurines and snap-on monster models. A special shelf held Peter's monster make-up: his fake blood, scar putty, fang teeth, bulging, bloodshot eyes, and finger nails like sabers. His door was framed with gruesome rubber Halloween masks, and white plastic skeletons dangled from the pulls of his window shades. From the ceiling hung forty assorted black rubber insects with waving feelers, trembling wings, and furred, springy legs.

Eliza's fur rose. "It gives me the shivers sometimes! And he's really such a nice little boy."

"He's forgotten to leave our breakfast," Eben pointed out, nosing along the rug.

"That's what I mean. All these monsters aren't good for him. Have you noticed that he's getting pale, Mr. Starbuck? And forgetful too."

"Well, Mrs. Starbuck, food isn't everything," Eben sighed reflectively.

He had good reason to remind Eliza of that, for it was a certain greed for food that had brought them all the way to New York. Eben and Eliza used to live in a lovely attic in a huge, old-fashioned house in Nantucket. They were rather old-fashioned mice themselves, with a long history of Nantucket ancestors, which is why they often called each other by their last names. But last summer they had gotten trapped in a grocery box and traveled all the way to New York City.

It took them weeks to find their way down along the maze of pipes in the huge and unfamiliar building. Thereafter no one knew they were in the building at all — until they came to Peter. In his apartment down on the fifth floor they found a delightful spot for a snug, warm home.

Eben chided her for being nervous. "You know enough about children, Eliza. It's just a passing phase. All we must do is keep out of sight."

It spite of all their precautions Peter saw them one night. He'd been in the middle of a terrible nightmare about two eyeless, headless blobs who were moving toward him with their armless, legless bodies. It frightened him so that he woke. Moonlight was streaming across the rug, and there, instead of the horrible dream-beings, he saw two tiny, soft-gray creatures with small round heads and bright, innocent eyes. Caught in the act of nibbling Oreo crumbs, Eben and Eliza had stood stock still, their tiny paws up, trembling.

Peter loved them on sight. He felt the little mice had saved him from some terrible disaster, and he took them to heart, feeding them, talking to them, watching over them. He didn't tell his mother or father— or even Obie and Sal—about his two new friends.

It wasn't long before Eben and Eliza grew to trust Peter. There was something in the way he left little things by their doorway that made them feel secure. Sometimes it would be only a small piece of cheese, a sandwich crust, or a bit of fruit. But often he brought them delicacies from the dinner table for a "midnight feast."

"There," he'd say, plunking down a morsel of chocolate cake. "You people have a party." Or he'd leave something strange, like long green strands of spinach, and whisper into their hole, "Eat it! It's terrible, but it's good for you. You need it in your diet."

Today was the first time Peter had ever forgotten them.

"What do you think it means, Mrs. Starbuck?" asked Eben disconsolately, as he looked around the cheeseless, cakeless, crumbless floor.

"It means this Monster Club is ruining a nice child," said Eliza. "It means we ought to help him."

"Help him!"

"Why yes, Mr. Starbuck. Peter has been very

kind to us. Without him, I don't know what we'd have done."

"We'd have made out," said Eben stoutly.

"But still..."

"Yes, still," said Eben after a moment. "You're right, Eliza. It would be good to help him if we could—but bless me if I know how."

"Well," said Eliza reasonably, "the first thing, obviously, would be to get rid of monster images. The pictures, the comics, the models, the masks."

Eben's eyes traveled over the room, from the cluttered shelves to the pictures lining the walls, and up to the ceiling—an enormous height—where the rubber bugs dangled far above his head. The view made him dizzy. "For us to get rid of all this, Eliza, would be like a human trying to remove a mountain."

"Humans say that faith moves mountains."

"A figure of speech, dear Eliza, that's all."

"I mean a little faith in what we *could* do."

Eliza hunched herself down on the rug to face the problem practically. "Suppose we nibbled a couple of pictures? Or just one? One we could get to, down below." Her whiskers quivered toward a magazine cover of Dracula that was pasted low, just above the baseboard moulding.

"Yes, we could gnaw at a picture or two," frowned Eben, "but what would it mean? Don't you realize, dear Eliza, that if we could tear every picture off every wall...if we could suddenly grow ten feet tall and rip the bugs from the ceiling...if we could dispose of every mask, model, and horror comic...that Peter would still have his monsters? They're in his mind, dear Eliza, in his *mind*."

"I suppose so," said Eliza, and shivered. "But isn't that all the more reason to make a start somewhere?"

"It's really his parents' business," said Eben. "They're the ones who ought to do something about it."

"Peter's parents haven't any idea what a serious problem it is. They think it's just a little club, a passing phase that'll go away." Eliza stared at Dracula, who gazed back evilly from the opposite wall. One arm held his black cape over half his face, and above it his eyes smiled in a sinister way.

"Please, Eben? Just one nibble at one picture? Peter will know we've done it — who else would chew up a picture? — and it'll be a sign."

"A sign of what?"

"Sort of a message from us, to let him know what we think."

"He'll probably think we were hungry!" Eben looked distastefully at Dracula. "Oh...all right."

Together they ran across the room.

"But if you think one picture will do it, Mrs. Starbuck, you're wrong. Another will just take its place. It isn't only Peter, remember, there's also Osbert."

"And Sal!" echoed Eliza. "I know. Never mind. Let's just start with Dracula."

"In a way," muttered Eben, "it's easier to face him than Sal."

He shuddered, but valiantly began to help Eliza with her "sign."

3

By the time school was over Peter was exhausted. As usual the monsters had been with him all day. Recently they'd started coming right into the classroom with him, where they'd hang about the walls, pretending to pick up education. Of course, they didn't. They were too dumb to learn anything. But they interfered with his books and papers, lost his pencils, distracted him from work. Today they'd even stolen his homework assignment. He knew it wasn't in his briefcase.

On his last report card Peter had received only one C—but lots of Ds and Fs. He was failing—all because of the monsters. As he walked down the steps Peter made up his mind. He was thoroughly sick of them.

Obie was waiting for him outside.

"Look, you go get the magazine today, Obie," said Peter. "I really feel sick."

"I'm sorry, Pete. Are you sure?"

"Positive."

Obie looked lost and unhappy.

"Why don't you meet Sal at her school?" suggested Peter. "Then you can get it together."

"Good idea!" Obie brightened. "We'll meet you back at the Club."

Peter watched Obie run up the street with the filched lunch money jangling in his pocket. He waited until he saw Obie turn the corner. The monsters were all over the street impatiently waiting for Peter. When he turned to go back into school, the Horde ran frantically after him.

"Where're you going?"

"School's over for the day!"

"You're supposed to go home now."

Peter ignored them. He walked through the entrance hall and opened the door to Chapel. The monsters jumped back in astonishment and milled about, bumping and lurching into each other. Bravely, Peter walked in.

As the door closed behind him, Peter sighed with relief. Peace! Quiet! Why hadn't he done this before?

Only one Sister was sitting in Chapel; the

French teacher for the fourth and fifth grades. When Peter came in and sat down in a prayerful attitude, she looked up in surprise. Quickly, she gathered her skirts and swept out. A child in Chapel. *After* school. A boy! And not just any boy — Peter James Wood who had that awful report card! Was there hope? She couldn't wait to tell Reverend Mother.

With Sister gone and the monsters safely outside, Peter relaxed so completely he almost fell asleep. Then he roused himself to do some hard thinking. He put his arms on the back of the seat before him, put his chin on his arms, and stared straight ahead.

Directly in front was the picture of the angel over the altar. It was a mural that one of the Sisters had painted almost entirely in gold. It was golden-gowned, golden-winged, with a bright golden halo. The wings were open, the hands outstretched, the toes pointed down in flight. The angel's face looked kind and calm and strong and wise.

An idea had been growing in Peter's mind all day:

"Maybe the way to get rid of monsters is to build an angel."

The minute Peter said the words out loud, he felt it was a grand idea. "Look how they never come into Chapel! If I have an angel at home they won't like it at all. They'll go away."

He thought a moment more.

"Even if they don't go away — if they make trouble or something — one angel can certainly handle a bunch of miserable monsters."

And that wasn't a cowardly thought, Peter reassured himself. What small boy could get rid of that horrible Horde all alone? But with a little help.... "It isn't as if I hadn't asked them to leave," he told the angel. "But they simply refuse to go!

"And they never bother Obie and Sal," he added, "only me."

Maybe that was because he'd had the monsters long *before* the Club, thought Peter. He was the one who was so crazy for monsters. When he started the Club, he was automatically President, because he already had such a terrific collection. He remembered the magazines and pictures beginning to grow around his bed and on his walls. He couldn't stop thinking about monsters, couldn't get enough monsters. Once he was even going to make a life-sized model, but he didn't need to, for the real ones appeared.

First it was just Frankie. And he hadn't been so bad, Peter reflected. They'd been quite good pals for awhile. But then Wolf Demon came, as company for Frankie, and then he got the Vampire, the Blue Blob, the Mud Men Twins, and the Giant Green Slug and Yellow Slime. So many of them were a nuisance, hanging around all day, but things hadn't really got out of hand until the night when the *others* came to call.

Peter shuddered, remembering how terrified he'd been. It was supposed to be just a little sleep-over with a few old friends, Frankie, Wolf Demon, and the Vampire. But it had turned into a monstrous slumber party.

Frankie, who was very possessive of Peter, wanted to sleep with him in the same bed. And Peter's bunk was narrow, so it was very crowded and uncomfortable. Frankie waved the others away to sleep on the top bunk, or the desk, or the floor. Actually, they could sleep in or on the walls, or in the air if they chose.

But they couldn't sleep, because they were bored. They murmured, growled, coughed, pretended to snore, acted like very bad children. Nights, they felt, were not for sleeping; nights were for fun, parties, mischief, for doing crazy, forbidden things. So taking advantage of Peter's hospitality they invited the others who arrived instantly and in throngs; drifting through the windows, crawling through cracks and crevices, snaking from under the floorboards, wafting through the walls.

"I didn't invite them," thought Peter unhappily. "I didn't even want them to come."

There were witches, warlocks, demons, furry beasts with fangs and claws, balls of fire, puffs of smoke, things made of clay and seaweed, molds and moss. Things that froze and boiled and slushed and dripped and oozed. They came to join the slumber party, and they stayed. They thought Peter was a real good sport. And they loved his room!

Now they popped up all the time, coming whenever they felt like it. Peter never knew when they'd choose to pay a visit, or choose to disappear.

"They have rotten manners," grumbled Peter. "If they didn't have rotten manners they'd leave when I asked them. Now I can't walk down a street without having something jump at me, push me, startle me, tickle me. Most of all I hate the ticklers.

"No," he corrected himself. "Most of all I hate never having any privacy! They never leave me alone!"

He sat up straight and stared at the angel.

"Isn't everybody supposed to have a guardian angel?" he inquired. "I've never seen mine. Maybe I don't have one. Does it matter? If I don't have one, I can always make one, can't I?"

He thought hard about making an angel. He could already visualize it completed. It would be just like that angel behind the altar, winged and golden and glowing, and kind and wise.

"And tough!" added Peter. "Tough enough to handle anything."

Now that he knew what to do, he didn't want to waste any time. He looked at his Charlie Tuna watch and figured quickly. Sal's school was three blocks away. By the time Obie met her, by the time they walked to the magazine store, by the time they stopped on every corner to look at pictures, by the time they finally wandered back to the Club in his room — he would have time to start. If he hurried now.

"Thanks," whispered Peter to the angel picture.

But it wasn't quite enough. He rose and saluted briskly. Then he marched out.

4

Although his pass was only for Broadway, Peter had a trick for getting on the Riverside Drive bus. He would flash his card so quickly the driver hardly had time to see it. Today the bus came so soon, and Peter was so fast that the Horde was almost left behind. They were upset with Peter for going into Chapel and furious about his bus maneuver. They'd thought he'd be walking home by the Drive. They had to leap for the windows and hang on outside.

Only Frankie managed to get in, and he hung by a strap, looking accusingly at Peter, who ignored him. In less than five minutes they were home.

Peter walked into the building trailing a long file of monsters behind him. He entered the elevator and momentarily they disappeared. They thought elevators were dumb. Only Frankie rode up with Peter to the fifth floor. When they got out, the hall was jam-packed with the others who had taken the easier way — drifting up the steps and through the walls. They crowded in around Peter as he dug through his pockets for his key.

Every day they made fun of this since to them, keys were senseless, useless objects. As Peter turned the key in the lock, raucous laughter filled the hall. Then they vanished again, but when Peter walked into his room they were waiting.

It was so crowded that Peter couldn't even see the pictures on his walls. Monsters were hanging from the ceiling, lying on the bookcases, draped across his desk, leaning on the window frames, sitting on his bureau. They were packed like giant sardines across his top bunk. And Wolf Demon was sprawled flat, arms behind his shaggy head, hogging the whole lower bunk and the pillow. Peter's own bed!

Angrily, Peter took hold of himself. "Never mind them, pay no attention."

He pushed his way across the room and with great difficulty managed to pull open his toy-closet door. He hadn't opened it in six months, and a great stack of games tumbled out and spilled on the floor. There was his old *Monopoly*, the red houses turning end over end. And *Go to the Head of the Class* — Peter blinked — with the counters rolling away on the rug. His old ship mobile fell out of its box. The thin threads that held the different types of sailing ships were all tangled and snarled. Peter gazed upon it wistfully. Once upon a time it had hung from his ceiling, instead of the rubber beetles and roaches and scorpions and centipedes and springy hairy tarantulas.

He kicked the boxes aside and reached into the dark closet for the light. It beamed over a floor filled with boxes of blocks and balls and skates and catcher's mitts. He pushed back, past forlorn objects hanging from hooks: his camping knapsack and canteen; his cowboy, sailor, and fireman hats; his old Halloween costumes of Snoopy and Casper the Ghost — how childish! Finally he found what he was after, wedged tightly in the rear, atop a large box of model trains.

Peter heaved and lifted and pulled, and finally dragged out an old, splintery, dust-covered barrel. Inside were coils of telephone cord, picture wire, clothes hangers, rolls of colored tape, a tin of rubber wheels off toys long since broken and discarded, and a round wicker sewing basket with a lid. He turned the barrel upside down and everything fell out. Then he rolled it on its side, and went to his desk drawer for a screwdriver, pliers, scissors, and a large hammer.

Once upon a time he had planned to make a very large monster from this barrel and everything inside it. "But now," Peter smiled for the first time that day, "you're going to become something quite, quite different."

He looked at the Horde defiantly. But they were bored with the toy closet, the barrel, and all the tools that had nothing to do with monsters. They shrugged, sniffed, wheezed, and suddenly disappeared.

"Aha!" Peter smiled again and took up his hammer.

"You see," he began to chat conversationally at the barrel, "I can't use you as you are because you're too heavy. I think angels have to be light."

Bang! He knocked out a slat and started on another. "Also you're too short and thick. I don't think angels are short and thick, they're tall and thin. So what I figure is. ..."

Bang! Another slat fell out, and Peter rolled the barrel again. "I'll just leave four or five staves and all the brass hoops for your body. That's from your chest to your legs. Then I have to make your shoulders and neck, arms and legs and head."

He sat cross-legged on the floor and pulled apart the wire hangers. There were dozens of them tied together with red plastic tape. He worked them out flat and straight with the pliers, and then wound two around the barrel hoop on top. "This is going to be your neck," he informed the barrel.

He drew the wires through the bottom of the round wicker basket. "And this is your head. Don't worry about your face, I'll get to that in a minute."

The wire hangers weren't quite strong enough to hold the basket head steady, so Peter added two more, making a very sturdy neck. "Now for your face," he said. "Think I'll do that before your arms and legs. You'd probably like to have a look around."

He poked through the tin of toy wheels for the nose and eyes, finding a small white one, and two larger black ones of the right size. Taking thin picture wire, he attached the wheels to the front of the basket, then stood back to survey his work.

"That looks good, but you need just the right mouth." He held up different rolls of the colored tape beneath the white wheel nose. But the red was too red, and pink was too pink—finally Peter settled on a light tan. He cut the tape in two pieces and attached it so the mouth was slightly open.

Then he began working on the arms and legs.

He made these from the thicker coil of white telephone cord, winding double lengths round and round for extra thickness. He made bendable knees and elbows by twining picture wire around the cord. Finally he cut twenty short lengths of cord for fingers and toes.

"I'm pretty sure angels have toes," he remarked. "And fingers. You're really going to need them for beating up the monsters. I mean, if angels beat up monsters. Maybe they don't. Maybe you can just ask them to leave and they'll go. They sure won't go for me."

"By the way," he added after a moment. "My name is Peter and I have a terrible monster problem."

5

Long ago Eben and Eliza had learned that if they were hungry, the best way not to be hungry was to sleep. So after chewing at Dracula they had slept all day. They woke to the noise of Peter's hammer and saw him pounding on the barrel slats, working with wire and cord, and talking cheerfully to himself. The picture was still hanging, torn, on the wall.

"I don't believe he's noticed it," said Eliza sadly.

"Well, at least he's not playing monsters." Eben peeked out their doorway. "He seems to be doing carpentry on that barrel."

"But he's forgotten our food *again*."

They waited by their small hole hungrily, hoping Peter would remember them. And a moment later in rushed Obie and Sal.

Obie had torn out half the pictures from the magazine and was waving them over his head. "Six full pictures of the Creature!" he shouted. "Let's put them next to the Giant Slug."

Sal's nose was buried in what was left of the magazine and she was so excited she was shuddering. "They're going to do a brand new movie about a mummy four thousand years old!" she cried, dropping right where she was on the floor.

Since Sal could wear anything she wanted to her school, she was wearing overalls, a plaid shirt, and striped baseball sneakers. Her yellow hair was long and straight and one of her front teeth was chipped. Sal liked to call that tooth her "fang." Whenever possible she displayed it, saying she was her own favorite monster.

"Ahhhh! Her name is Altathea and they call her The Frozen Brain," sighed Sal happily.

"Why is that so wonderful?" Obie looked over her shoulder at the picture of Altathea.

"Because when she thaws out, her brain remembers being frozen. So she can freeze anybody else in the world with just a wave of her hand."

Sal waved her own hand, pretending to be Altathea. "Freeze!" she commanded Peter.

But Peter kept right on making toes.

Obie finally noticed. He saw the barrel with the basket head, the cord and wire, the broken slats. "Say!" he looked at Peter working, "I thought you were sick."

"I am," said Peter, attaching another toe to one leg. It bothered him a little that the angel didn't have feet. The white cord legs just dripped down and went straight into five knotted, lumpy toes. But he didn't know what he could do about it.

What bothered him even more though, was what he now had to tell Obie and Sal. He could lie, and say he was making something different — even a monster—but he didn't think it would be fair to the angel. This was almost the worst moment of his day. He would have to tell the truth.

"I am sick," said Peter, taking a deep breath. "I'm sick of monsters."

Obie and Sal were too astonished to speak.

"So, I…I'm making an angel," added Peter bravely.

"An angel!" spluttered Sal.

Obie looked at the barrel closely. He found his voice. "You mean one of those fallen angels?" He explained to Sal, "We heard about them in Religious Knowledge class. Sister said there are supposed to be over three hundred thousand angels, and lots of 'em are bad. Satan's the head of them all. He was an angel too, you know, when he started."

"No, I didn't know," said Sal with interest.

"Is that what you're making, Pete?" implored Obie hopefully. "A devil angel?"

No, I'm making a good one."

"*Why?*" cried Obie and Sal.

"Because ... because the monsters have been giving me nightmares," explained Peter truthfully. (Even if it was only half the truth.)

"I thought you liked having nightmares!" cried Obie. "You said you liked to be shivery and scary and everything."

"I used to," said Peter heavily.

"Pete, you don't mean that you don't want to be in the Club anymore!" said Obie in an agonized way.

"Well," began Peter slowly, "not unless...unless we could have a different sort of club."

"Not an angel club!" shouted Obie.

"Oh, no!" yelled Sal. "We'd have to be so good all the time. It wouldn't be any fun!"

"You can't stop now, Pete," cried Obie. "There's going to be a monster convention next month. It's listed in the magazine. We can go, we can get back issues, they'll have so many old horror comics."

Peter shook his head.

Sal was staring around the room at the pictures,

masks, and models. "We could take them up to my house," she suggested. "But listen, Obie, if we move the Club up there I get to be President. I'll make myself a mummy case and I can lie in it and pretend to be Altathea."

Desperately Obie tried again. "Pete, if you won't be in the Club anymore, you know what you will be? Chicken-sissy! A miserable, weak, faint-hearted, lily-livered chicken-sissy!"

Peter winced, but he had sort of expected this.

"Building an angel's a chicken thing to do. Chicken, chicken, chicken!"

"I could have told you I was making a monster," retorted Peter. "I don't think telling the truth is as chicken as lying."

Obie looked at Peter with disgust. "You sound just like one of the Sisters. A real sissy Sister."

"Then think of me like that!" Peter yelled back. "Think of me as a sissy Sister!"

"He doesn't sound like that to me," observed Sal. "He sounds kind of strong to me."

Obie was marching to the door.

"Shall we take everything to my house?" urged Sal.

"You'd have to ask your parents first," Peter reminded her. He said to Obie, "It's too bad your parents won't let you have the monsters. I know how much you love them."

Obie stopped at the door with a down-turned mouth. "I'll be in touch," he said. "Later. When we figure out what to do."

"Yes, do stay in touch, Obie," said Peter, feeling awful. He hadn't quarreled with Obie for a long, long time.

Obie, with a grim face, stalked out. Sal lifted down the sign that had hung on Peter's door for the past year, and tucked it under her arm. It read:

PRIVATE—KEEP OUT
THIS IS A CLUB FOR MONSTERS ONLY
THAT MEANS YOU

When they had gone Peter thought of broken dreams, of lost friendships, of all the fun they'd had together in the Club — at first. He gazed wistfully at the monsters' clutter of his room. "If you had only stayed just pictures on the walls," he began.

And as his view swept the assorted horrors, he suddenly noticed the picture of Dracula down near the baseboard. It was all ripped and torn and hanging by one old piece of scotch tape. Obie hadn't been near it, and neither had Sal. Peter was certain it had been in one piece this morning. He bent to examine it closely. It seemed to have been *chewed*.

"Oh!" he cried, feeling suddenly awful. He had forgotten *again*! "I'm so sorry!"

He knelt by the mousehole near his bureau. "I didn't mean to forget you this morning — and I did remember later." He dug into his pocket for the bread crumbs he'd saved from lunch. "And I'll try to bring you a treat from dinner — something to make up for forgetting."

Peter stood up sighing. To think they were so hungry they'd gnawed on *paper*.

But as he turned back to work on the barrel, Peter suddenly frowned. Mice didn't eat paper when they were hungry — did they? They had excellent eyesight—didn't they? That picture was pretty horrible! He couldn't imagine even a mouse nibbling on Dracula.

He whirled around again and caught a swift glimpse of vanishing pink tails. The crumbs were gone. They were so fast! And probably very clever too.

He stared at their small doorway, wondering aloud. "Unless...maybe you didn't chew up that picture because you were hungry at all. Maybe you just don't like monsters! Were you trying to tell me something?"

There was no answer, of course, but the idea made Peter more eager than ever to finish his angel. "Well, don't worry about it," he called over his shoulder as he sat down again by the barrel. "I'm as sick of 'em as you are! And we're going to get rid of 'em for once and for all.

"A wonderful, tough, golden angel!" muttered Peter, starting to work on the other toes.

6

As she watched and listened to Peter, Eliza was horrified. "You can never tell about children," she said.

Eliza often said that, from long experience of her own children, her grandchildren, and the children of the summer renters in Nantucket. Now she was so upset that she repeated herself with feeling.

"You can never tell about children, Eben. But my guess is that Peter has gone mad."

"He seems very calm to me," said Eben. "Very busy, building, working, quite content."

"That was not my meaning. What I meant was crazy. Mad in the sense of crazy. We never knew a crazy child before, did we?"

Eben sifted back through his memories of all the summer children, giving the question long consideration. "There was the Hooper child," he said at last.

"Oh yes, the red-haired one with the laboratory."

"He was not content," reflected Eben. "He made bombs."

"Yes, so he did. But the bombs didn't go off," she reminded Eben. "They fizzled."

"Thank the good Lord!" said Eben.

"And the Hooper child wasn't crazy," said Eliza, looking pointedly at Peter.

"I don't believe Peter is crazy either," remarked Eben thoughtfully.

"But look at him out there!" exclaimed Eliza. "Hovering over that object, babbling to himself."

"It's not an object, dear Eliza, it's a barrel. And he's not babbling to himself; he's babbling to the barrel which is about to become an angel."

"Oh, that is not an angel, Mr. Starbuck!" Now Eliza had come to the heart of her discontent and she quivered all over. "That is not, and cannot ever be, an angel!"

"How do you know that, Mrs. Starbuck? Have you ever seen an angel?"

"Yes!" Eliza bristled, as she did when she felt put-upon. "Yes, I have. There was a picture of an angel in the downstairs bedroom in Nantucket."

"I mean a *real* angel," prodded Eben.

"Well...no," confessed Eliza.

42

"There!" said Eben triumphantly. "So how do you know that barrel is not already an angel—in disguise?"

Eliza sniffed. "I refuse to answer you. Because if I do, I may have to decide there are two crazies here."

Eben hunched himself down in a settled manner, crossed his paws and stared at his wife. As he had said many times before, he said again, "Eliza, I simply don't understand you."

As she had said many times before, Eliza replied, "Why not?"

Eben outlined the situation for her. "One, Peter is not playing monsters, he is doing something creative and good. He is carpentering an angel. Two, he did not forget to feed us. Three, he finally observed the picture of Dracula. Four, he not only observed it, Eliza, he actually said, out loud, in our hearing, that perhaps we were trying to 'tell him something.'

"Everything, Mrs. Starbuck, *everything* has turned out exactly as you hoped and wished. And now you say that poor child is crazy. I simply don't understand you."

"His head is just too stuffed with monsters," said Eliza. "Wait and see."

A shaft of afternoon sunlight fell across the rug where Peter was working, and caught the dust

motes in the air. Peter sneezed, and a deep, hollow voice said, "Gesundheit."

Wolf Demon materialized to breathe over Peter's shoulder. "What 'cha doing?" he asked curiously.

Peter hesitated. Then he thought—oh well. By now anybody in his right mind could see what it was—"I'm making an angel," said Peter.

"What's that?" asked Wolf Demon.

"It's something...something...well, I don't know how to describe it. Anyway, I don't think you'd understand."

"Is it another monster like me?" asked Wolf Demon hopefully.

"No," said Peter. "It's quite, quite different."

"Then why're you making it?" He leaned his furry head on Peter's shoulder. His pointed ears tickled and his head was heavy and uncomfortable. His fangs dripped unpleasantly near Peter's neck.

"I'm making it so that you will leave," said Peter.

"Oh?" Wolf Demon examined the barrel body and the basket head, the black rubber wheel eyes, white nose, the taped mouth, and the telephone cord arms and legs. "Oh, yeah," he chuckled, "sure."

Behind the baseboard Eliza squeaked in terror. "I didn't see Obie come back in."

"He…he…he…d-d-didn't!" stuttered Eben.

"Then who…who came in…in a Halloween costume?" asked Eliza faintly.

"Halloween has long since come and gone," replied Eben in a wobbling voice. "That is not a child in a Halloween costume, Mrs. Starbuck. We were both wrong. Peter hasn't gone mad. He not only thinks his monsters are real — they *are* real! Look…look…oh, look there!"

The rest of the Horde suddenly appeared to join Wolf Demon, and surrounded Peter in a hideous semicircle as he worked on the floor.

"Ohohohohoh," Eliza's teeth chattered while her fur rose like an electric halo. Eben moved closer and they huddled together, shivering with fear.

Eben and Eliza crept to a dark corner of their home and hid in the shadow.

Then, Eliza began bustling about, sweeping bits of dust fluff with her tail toward their door.

"What are you doing, Eliza?"

"Oh, please help, Eben. We must close our door."

"Of course!" Eben sighed. "Perhaps I could make us a monster-proof door, dear Eliza, like the one we had in our attic?"

Back in Nantucket Eben had made a lovely door from the lid of a can of peaches. It wasn't to protect them from monsters, of course, but from the renters' children and their many dogs and cats.

All that seemed long ago, but Eben felt valiant again. "If I go out scouting for a can, Eliza, the monsters won't even know we're here."

"That won't be necessary, Mr. Starbuck," said Eliza kindly, "since we're not going to be here."

"I can understand why you'd want to move to another home," said Eben, dreading the prospect of another journey through the building. "But we are getting a little old for all this exploration."

"Old or not, Mr. Starbuck, prepare to leave the building."

"The building!" Eben's whiskers twitched and his eyes grew dim. "We don't have to do that, Eliza. We can just move to another floor."

"No, we can't, Mr. Starbuck. I'm sure there's no church here on any floor."

"Church!" cried Eben.

"Why, yes. We have to get to a church, Mr. Starbuck."

"What *for*?"

"To find a real angel for Peter, of course, instead of that...*thing*...out there."

"Eliza, you've gone mad!" Eben sagged heavily on the floor. "We've never even seen the first floor," he whispered hoarsely. "You've heard the children talk. There's a huge city out there with streets and cars and lights and noise and confusion. We can't leave the building!"

"We have to." She gazed at him steadily. "Where else would you expect to find a real angel—if not in some church somewhere?"

"What makes you think Peter's angel won't pop up here — at any moment?" asked Eben. "Why must we go find it?"

"Because we must," answered Eliza mysteriously. Then she joked, "Oh, buck up, Mr. Starbuck, and help me close our door. We have to let Peter know we're away. If we vanished without leaving a sign it would make him very unhappy."

Eben looked at her for a long time. He crept back to peek at the barrel. The Horde had gone and Peter had gone to dinner. He stared at the weird-looking object on the floor, trying to see it as an angel. It was easier when he wasn't looking directly at it.

He pondered slowly, thinking of Peter and that barrel — angel. "As you say, we are old. We could stay and look after ourselves. But perhaps it's not a time for that."

Eben's eyes began to gleam. "You're a brave lady, Eliza Starbuck! You're a little like I imagine one of those old ship captains would have been. You have a way of inspiring people. I've always liked that about you, Eliza."

48

"Thank you, Mr. Starbuck."

"And it's not a bad thing for an old mouse to try and help a little boy, is it? The idea makes me feel young again."

"It will be a glorious adventure, Eben!" whispered Eliza.

"But a real angel..." Eben frowned. "We just might be able to find a church — but an honest-to-goodness angel, Eliza?"

"Oh, I believe we can find one," she said. "I believe you can find almost anything — if you look."

7

Obie felt terrible. His best friend, Peter James Wood, to suddenly give up the Monster Club, just like that! Obie sat down on a chair in Sally's "junk" room. It was right off the kitchen and contained an old mattress, a rickety table, a broken-down baby carriage, extra air conditioners, boxes, suitcases, and dozens of empty picture frames.

Sal was leaping about and exclaiming, "We could frame all the pictures! We could use the table for a model shelf. I could make the mummy case on top of the mattress! And look, there's even a little bathroom. We could put blue lights inside, and wallpaper it with monster posters!"

Obie just sat glumly, chin between his hands. Sal felt awful too. It wouldn't be much fun without Peter, with just the two of them.

"Maybe we could get some other people to join the Club," she suggested.

"I don't think I care about the Club anymore," said Obie.

"I guess I don't either." Sal plopped down on the mattress. "But without the Club — without monsters — what'll we *do*?"

"I guess I'll go play ball or something," said Obie.

Oh, dear! thought Sal. If he went out to play ball, that would be the end of everything. She knew boys. Obie would play ball — or something — every day, and she'd be left all alone.

"Obie, would you like to have a Brain Club instead?"

"Oh, brains, brains, you and your brains!"

"I made a whole bunch of them this summer and they're fascinating!" cried Sal. "You have no idea how great they can be."

But Obie had picked up his things and was heading for the door. "You can keep all the magazines," he said.

"Did you know that if you tickle one part of a brain you can remember everything?" asked Sal. "Everything that ever happened to you."

"Good-bye, Sal." Obie went out to the hall, and Sal trailed after him.

"*Obie!*" she suddenly shrieked so loudly that he stopped. "You know what we could do? We could make a brain for Peter's angel!"

Obie wrinkled his nose.

"No! Listen! We never made a brain for a monster, did we?"

"No," said Obie.

"Think how much more fascinating an angel's brain would be. Can you imagine what an angel thinks about?"

Obie winced. This sounded too much like school. "They think about sweet things all the time."

"Maybe they don't!" cried Sal. "How do you know?"

"I know," said Obie, although he didn't, really. "Anyway I'm not interested in angels. Or brains."

Sal grabbed his arm. "There's another thing," she whispered, "How's Peter going to bring that angel to life?"

"What do you mean?"

"We never built a monster and brought it to life, did we?"

"No...."

"Well, here's our chance!"

"It's not a monster," said Obie. "It's an angel."

"Yes, but it's got to be brought to life just the same. How did Dr. Frankenstein bring his monster to life?"

Obie's eyes opened wide. "With lightning."

"Right!" said Sal excitedly. "And we could help Peter bring his angel to life the same way. At night, a dark, stormy night...."

"With lightning...."

"On the roof...."

"And he'll fly away...."

"Just like a monster!"

"But he *will* be an angel?" asked Obie suspiciously. Sometimes he didn't quite trust Sal. As disappointed as he was with Peter, he didn't think it would be quite fair to have the angel turn out to be a monster.

"Of course, it'll be an angel!" said Sal. "I'm going to make his brain, aren't I?"

Obie looked at her. His books and coat were getting heavy. "Open the door," he said. "Please?"

Sal opened the front door and Obie stepped out to the hall. "Aren't I?" she insisted.

"Well...okay," said Obie. "You make the brain if you want to, and I...I'll think about the rest of it."

Sal was so happy she did cartwheels all the way down the hall and into her room.

8

Peter was alone in his room after dinner, since the Horde had left "to attend a meeting somewhere," they'd said. Peter hoped they'd stay away all night for a change.

"You still need hair, wings, a gown, and a halo," he said to the angel. "Hair first."

He knew where his mother kept an extra mop, and brought it back to his room. He took the mop off the pole and attached it with picture wire to the basket head. Long strands of dirty gray cotton dripped all over the face and hung unevenly down the barrel back. Peter cut it as he thought an angel's hair should be, shoulder length, with bangs in front. But it still didn't look much like angel hair.

"Something to wear might help," he said. With all the wire and cord sticking out, it looked rather mechanical and freakish.

"I wonder if mother would give me one of her old nightgowns?" He hated to ask because he didn't want to say what it was for. He could say he was making *The Bride of Frankenstein*, but somehow he didn't think his mother would like that.

Maybe the angel wouldn't like it either.

"No nightgown," he decided. "Anyway, it would make you look too girlish. You're not a girl angel. You've got to be a strong guy, like Michael or Gabriel."

They were the only two angel names that Peter knew, and it gave him a new problem. "I don't know what to call you. Maybe just Angel — or *Mr.* Angel will do."

He went out to the hall closet and rummaged around. It was filled with miscellaneous boots, coats, umbrellas, old boxes, and shopping bags. He found a tan raincoat that his father hadn't worn in some time. The pockets were ripped and there was a stain down one side. Peter didn't think his father would ever miss it. He draped it around the barrel body and pulled the cord arms through the sleeves.

The sleeves were much too long, so Peter cut them off. The coat was too long too, so he cut off the bottom all around. In spite of the bulging barrel, the coat was also too large. Peter took the long belt from his tan bathrobe and tied it round the middle.

The angel began to look like a spy. The black wheel eyes almost looked like dark glasses. The nose was strange, the mouth seemed to sneer. Peter stood back, frowning. What was wrong? With the cord toes and fingers drooping from the raincoat, the lumpy mop hair dripping on his neck, those rubber eyes staring, it looked very, very peculiar.

"You look like another monster," said Peter suddenly. "You don't look like the angel I had in mind at all."

Obie stood by his window on the ninth floor. Outdoors a wild wind was blowing and bending the tops of the trees in the park. Sal did have good ideas sometimes. It would be wonderful to take Peter's angel up to the roof on a stormy night and watch it fly away. He wondered what Peter would use for wings. If he made them strong enough, maybe it really would fly.

But why did Peter have to make an angel! Why couldn't it be a winged monster instead? That would be twice as exciting. They could all have fun, scaring themselves silly.

Obie remembered going to the Cathedral once with Peter and pretending it was a huge horror castle. Ghosts and demons lurked in every corner, each footfall was an approaching menace, and at any moment, they had thought, the statues and pictures and gargoyles would come to life and turn their heads. They'd sat frozen in delicious fear, with chills running up and down their spines.

But you certainly wouldn't have any chills with an angel! How did Peter get so sissy all of a sudden?

"Oh, well," thought Obie. If Peter didn't like being scared anymore, there wasn't any reason why Obie couldn't enjoy himself. He'd have to talk Peter into taking that thing up to the roof, but Obie was sure he could do that. And once they got it up there — well, let Peter have his old angel. Obie could always pretend it was a monster instead.

"Besides," thought Obie, "Sal is making a brain for it. If I know Sal, she'll never be able to make an angel's brain!"

And Sal was having trouble with the brain. She sat at her desk working with a glob of clay. She moistened it with water and kneaded it and pounded. She'd propped a book up on the desk with a picture of the human brain. She always used it as a model. But now the idea of copying a human brain bothered her.

"Angels couldn't be anything like humans," muttered Sal uncomfortably. "I wonder what they are like?"

All around her room, Sal's shelves were filled with interesting clay sculptures. She'd made some very pretty pots and bowls and exotic-looking animals, too. But all this year she'd been interested only in brains. To become a brain surgeon was the most wonderful thing she could imagine. To Sal a brain wasn't ugly, it was beautiful. Every little ridge and groove meant something special. There were areas for speech and hearing, movement — and those fascinating areas for memory.

One of Sal's shelves held nothing but the brains she'd made to scale in Nantucket. They were all in a row, neatly labeled: Brain of a Dunce, Brain of a Queen, Brain of an Astronaut, Brain of an Artist, Brain of a Mad Scientist. Each was made just a little differently, and each was Sal's original invention.

"But how to invent an angel's brain?" wondered Sal. "What would an angel remember? What does an angel *do*?"

She definitely needed information. She wiped her hands and got out her dictionary.

ANGEL: *A supernatural messenger of God ...*

superior to man in power and intelligence ...(Oh, that would be hard, Sal frowned.) ...*hence a messenger, as of spring or death ... also applied to an evil being of similar powers....*

An evil being! Sal jumped! She closed the book. So that was what Obie had meant about bad angels. It would be so easy to make a bad one. She could do it just like she'd done the Mad Scientist. Just mix everything up. She could switch the grooves for pleasure and pain.

But that wouldn't be fair, thought Sal. Peter wanted a good angel. If only she knew more about them. The dictionary certainly didn't tell her much, just "messenger." What kind of messenger would he be?

"Why am I saying it's a *he* angel?" Sal asked herself. "Maybe it's a girl. Are angels boys or girls? The dictionary didn't say anything about that. Maybe they're in-between, like me?

Yes, that was a start. She would definitely make an in-between brain. Sal worked the clay into a nice round shape and sighed. If only she were making the brain of Altathea. An Egyptian Princess, and a mummy, at that! There wouldn't be any problem with memory — Sal knew exactly what she'd do. She'd leave in the memory of being frozen and wipe everything else right out. Whereas Peter's angel should remember who it was, and what it had done, and something about Peter as well. It was going to be so hard....

"Oh dear," sighed Sal, beginning to work. Her fingers moved over the clay as her thoughts flitted back and forth between monsters and angels, mad scientists and poor, frozen Altathea.

"Anyway, it'll be a brain!" muttered Sal.

9

It was after dark when Eben and Eliza scurried out the basement door and darted for the shelter of a garbage can in the courtyard. Eliza's small heart was beating fast and Eben had a hard time catching his breath.

It had been a terrible journey down from the fifth floor. Twice they'd been lost and had to retrace their steps. Finally they found a way down alongside a hot water pipe that led to a small sink in the basement. They got out through a crack where the sink joined the wall, but had to walk right across the hot pipe. Eben had scorched his feet and Eliza singed the fur on her stomach.

The cold wind blowing from the river made them shiver. "We'd better keep going," cried Eliza.

"But where? Which way?" asked Eben.

Beyond an iron fence was a sidewalk and then a narrow street. On the other side feathery tree limbs reached into a sky that held only faint traces of a purple sunset. Somewhere in the distance was the hum of traffic. "It almost sounds like the sea," said Eliza.

Suddenly a car raced past them up the narrow street, and they jumped. At the same time there was a clatter in the courtyard. They turned to see the superintendent coming out with another garbage can on a dolly.

"Run, Eben!" Eliza flashed between the fence railings with Eben close behind. "Stick to the shadows," he called.

When they reached the corner the wind was blowing harder. They huddled next to the building, peeking around. On their left was the dark parkland of Riverside Drive. Ahead and above were masses of huge apartment buildings, so high they couldn't even see the roofs. "They must be skyscrapers," shouted Eliza over the wind, "and I don't see a church steeple anywhere."

"Maybe there *aren't* any churches in New

York!" Eben called wildly. "It doesn't seem like a place for them."

"Peter speaks of his class going to a cathedral," he said, more calmly. "A cathedral sounds larger than a church to me."

"Yes, that's what we want!" cried Eliza. "If it's large it may have a large angel. Do you know where this cathedral is?"

"No, but Peter's class walks there from school."

"Which way is Peter's school, Mr. Starbuck?"

"I don't know, Eliza, but sometimes he takes the Broadway bus."

"Which way is Broadway, Mr. Starbuck?"

"Oh, Eliza, I don't know any more than you do!" Eben panted impatiently. The wind was whipping so fiercely it blew all his fur to one side and almost took his breath away. "I don't know where anything is. But it must be a street, and I don't think it's that way—" He pointed in the direction of the park.

"Then we'll go the other way," she cried, "and find this street called Broadway!"

They waited until the street seemed clear, then scurried swiftly across, where they stopped in the lee of a waste paper basket. Eliza said, "Look Eben." She was observing a woman who stood on the opposite corner waiting for the light to change. "I think we were wrong, Mr. Starbuck.

She waits until that light changes. That is what we must do."

But when they saw what lay ahead, they hesitated. At the end of the next block was a confusion of blinking lights and hurrying people. "Perhaps it's Broadway!" cried Eliza.

They crept ahead, dazzled by the lights and the noise. Horns blared, sirens wailed, the footsteps of so many people sounded like armies on the march. Hugging the sides of the buildings, they reached the corner and darted into some dark shadows between two boxes standing in front of a store. People were going in and out of the doors. When Eben noticed they went in empty handed but came out carrying huge paper bags, he panicked.

"Eliza! This is a grocery store! And we are standing between two grocery cartons!"

They looked up at the walls of cardboard and trembled, remembering what had happened the last time they were near a grocery box. Eliza shifted her gaze to the wide, dangerous street. Then she noticed a sort of island in the center of the street. A place with trees, where the traffic divided.

"I think we can make it to the middle, Eben, and we must get out of here!"

Two huge legs moved threateningly near the

64

cartons. Eliza forgot her own warning about waiting for lights to change. She darted out so quickly that Eben had no chance to stop her. She ran right between the legs of a woman who was so startled that she screamed — and dropped her bag of groceries.

Apples and oranges rolled across the sidewalk. A carton of eggs broke right at the woman's feet. She slipped and fell down. Out in the street two cars suddenly slammed on their brakes with a horrible screeching sound. The drivers thought they'd seen a gray shadow flash in front of their wheels.

Eliza had disappeared!

Eben couldn't see Eliza anywhere. And he couldn't move out from the cartons because a crowd of people had gathered around the fallen woman.

"Are you hurt?" they asked.

"No," she said faintly, "but there are creatures in this store."

Eben looked at the people, he peered out at the street. He was terrified that Eliza had been crushed by the terrible speeding cars. His heart was going a mile a minute and he thought his head would burst. "I am too old for all this," thought Eben.

But he watched for the light to change. Just as the woman was pulled to her feet it turned. Eben dashed out, right between her legs again. Fainting, she fell back into the arms of her rescuers. "Creatures, creatures," she moaned, and called for the store manager.

Eben zipped across the street and leaped up to the divider in the middle. He found a wooden bench with stone sides. Behind the bench was a very messy and littered island of earth and faded grass. Eben scurried behind, and there, twitching and shaking from head to toe, was Eliza!

They fell upon each other with squeaks of terror and thanksgiving. "Mrs. Starbuck, don't you ever do that again!"

"Oh, Eben, I won't!" cried Eliza. "I thought I was going to be run over."

"So did I. A squashed heap."

"Oh, Eben!"

"Oh, Eliza!"

They waited for their small hearts to stop pounding and then looked around. On either side traffic was zooming up and down, past rows of shops and lights and people.

"Think of it, Eben. We're sitting in the middle of Broadway!" sighed Eliza.

"I think I would rather be sitting in the middle of those monsters," said Eben. "And we are not going to walk up Broadway looking for a church, Mrs. Starbuck. I don't care what you say. This street is just too dangerous."

"I agree. We'll have to find another one."

"Very well," Eben agreed reluctantly. "But this time wait for the light, Eliza. And *walk*. Don't dash."

It was cold going up the next block to Amsterdam Avenue. There wasn't as much wind, but there was an icy chill in the air. The street was lined with old tenements and brownstones, and was dark, bleak, and almost deserted.

"Not so many shops here," said Eben, shivering, as they reached the corner. "And the street should be easier to cross, because all the traffic is going one way."

"That is very observant of you, Mr. Starbuck," said Eliza, huddling at the bottom of some steps to look around. And then she gave a little cry, "Oh, Eben, look! I never thought we'd find one so soon."

Across the street, on the northeast corner was a large gray building with a high pointed tower.

"It's a church steeple, isn't it Eben?"

"I don't know," he peered at it doubtfully. "It doesn't look like the one at home, in Nantucket."

"Let's find out, Mr. Starbuck," said Eliza, and they hurried across the street. Outside the large gray building an iron gate stood open, and up a flight of steps was an open door. A soft, warm light spilled out in a welcoming way.

They crept past the gate, up the steps, and peeked in to see a bright red carpet stretching away under rows of red plush seats.

"I don't know if it's really a church or not," said Eliza. "I don't see an angel anywhere."

"Maybe they're way inside, Eliza," said Eben, wanting to get in from the cold. "But it's up to you, Mrs. Starbuck. In or out?"

"In!" said Eliza, and they whisked in under the rows of seats.

A moment later they heard voices behind them. "Good night, sir," said someone. "Good night," came the reply. They heard doors being closed and locked, and then soft footsteps fading away.

"We're certainly in," said Eben. "Whatever this is, I think they've locked up for the night."

The lights went out suddenly, and there was then a deep, complete silence. Eben and Eliza grew aware of a soft glow coming from somewhere beyond the rows of seats. They crept forward slowly toward the light. There, on top of a long table covered with purple cloth, they found two bright candles burning on either side of a golden cross.

"I don't know," said Eliza slowly. "We've never

been inside a church, as you say. But this *feels* right somehow, doesn't it, Eben?"

"Indeed it does," he whispered, looking up.

"Then there ought to be an angel!" she said, turning around to search. The seats swept back in a wide circle and above, in some sort of a balcony, she saw an enormous instrument—it was an organ—with ivory and gold-colored pipes. "But there isn't an angel anywhere!"

"Oh, yes there is—there *are*!" cried Eben. "I've found four of 'em."

Eliza hurried to look. He had discovered four tiny pictures high on the wall, two on either side of the central altar. She crawled up to the top of a seat and strained forward to examine their faces.

In one picture a figure was holding a jar, in another a crown, another held a box, and the last was simply kneeling. Eliza leaned so far forward she nearly toppled off the seat.

Finally she crawled down and crept slowly to the foot of the altar. There she sat, put two tiny pink paws over her small gray head, and started to cry.

"What on earth is the matter, dear Eliza? They have wings! Aren't they angels?"

"Oh, yes," she sobbed, "they're angels all right. Don't think I don't know an angel when I see one!"

"Then what *is* it, Eliza?" urged Eben.

"They're not the right angels for Peter," she

wept. "They couldn't help him one bit!"

"Why not, Mrs. Starbuck?" asked Eben, mystified.

"Just look at their faces and you'll see. They're not only too small, they're far too dreamy and *sweet*!"

10

At the same time that Eliza was crying by the altar,
Peter was kneeling by her old front door. As he
put down the brownie crumbs he'd saved from
dinner, he noticed that the mouse hole was stuffed
with dustballs. Frantically Peter pulled out the
fluff and called for his friends.

"Hello there? Are you there? Why did you plug
up your hole? Please come out!"

He waited. What mouse could resist that delicious brownie smell? But there were no mice. He
called again. He got his flashlight and beamed it
into their empty home. Peter couldn't see very far
inside, but it looked dark and gloomy. There

wasn't a sign of a bright eye or flickering tail. They had gone!

He looked at the bits of fluff on the floor. Did mice always plug up their doors when they went away? Or was that just another "message" to him, like the ripped picture of Dracula? It seemed to Peter the mice were saying, "We don't like monsters, and we don't like you, either. Good-bye forever."

Tears rolled down Peter's cheeks. "If only you'd waited," he said to the absent mice. "I told you it was going to be all right."

He didn't care if it was sissy to cry. He'd lost everything now. His best friend Obie, Sal, and now even his special pals, the mice. He felt all shaky and empty inside, as if it were the end of the world. Next thing he might even lose himself. He certainly didn't feel like working on the angel.

Peter sat on the edge of his bunk and stared at it. The barrel was sitting on the floor, leaning against a leg of his desk. The legs stuck straight out, the arms and hands sprawled beside them. The tape mouth had a funny, crooked grin, and the rubber wheel eyes seemed to be mocking him.

How come when you started to do something good, wondered Peter, all these horrible things happened?

And who cared about an old angel anyhow?

As he sat, chin between his hands, the Horde began to reappear. They popped up like balloons being pricked in reverse. Prick! A monster appeared in a bubble of air. Prick! Another monster. And another, and another....

"Did ya miss us, sissy boy?" asked Wolf Demon in a simpering voice.

"Did ya, did ya, did ya?" The rest echoed, giggling horribly.

The Mud Men gurgled and slurped in a mincing little waltz around the room. "We're chicken-sissies just like Peter, ha, ha, ha!"

"How's that chicken-sissy angel coming along?" grinned the Vampire with his red teeth.

"Going to make an angel, an angel, an angel!" They all clasped paws and talons and claws and did a foolish little circle dance around the room.

"We know what an angel is now," Wolf Demon leered at Peter. "Guess where we found out! And you'll be sorry."

"Sorry, sorry! Sissy, sissy!" they all sang.

Peter shuddered. Their voices grated terribly when they got excited.

"Know what you ought to call that angel?" someone croaked. "Sister Angel!"

"Sister Sissy Angel!" They rumbled and wheezed, and stood around jeering.

"That's some angel."

"Now isn't that a pretty thing?"

"It looks worse than me."

"HAW, HAW, HAW!"

"Where do you suppose that dumb angel's from?"

"Ooh, la, la! It's from Heaven, of course."

"What's that?"

"That place."

"Where is it?"

"Ooh, you know. Up there, somewhere."

"*Where?* Up or down?"

"Are you kidding, Sissy Beastie? You know there ain't no difference between up and down."

"*Isn't* any...."

"Ain't."

"*Isn't!* Watch your language. We been to Peter's school now.

"Hey! If that angel's from Heaven, I'm from Hell!"

"HAW, HAW, HAW!" The room exploded with laughter.

The more they joked, the worse Peter felt. The angel did look terrible, just awful. Everything he'd tried to make it look better only made it look worse.

Frankie lurched to the bunk and laid his huge gloved hand on Peter's shoulder. "We got a message for you, kid. Sort of from higher up."

"HA, HA, HEE, HEE!"

"QUIET!" roared Frankie at the others. "The message is this, kid. That barrel ain't never going to be no angel."

"*Any* angel," someone wheezed.

"SIMMER DOWN!" shouted Frankie, then whispered in Peter's ear, "You got the whole thing mixed up, kid. That angel's no friend of yours. *We're* your friends, see?"

"What you ought to do, Pete," said Wolf Demon cheerfully, "is turn that thing into a real nice monster. A good pal, you know, like one of us."

He wouldn't have to *turn* it into anything, thought Peter, staring at the barrel. Just as it was it would make a terrific monster.

He looked at the abandoned mouse hole. Everyone had left him. Nobody cared. He didn't really want another monster, but maybe Frankie and Wolf Demon were right.

What other friends did he have now?

It was one of the worst nights of Peter's life. The monsters didn't leave him alone for a minute. When he went to bed they invaded his room, bringing even more creatures than they had to that long-ago slumber party.

And when Peter finally fell asleep, he had a hideous nightmare about his angel. He dreamed

that some sort of meeting was in progress—in his room—and that the angel was asking the Horde to leave.

"LEAVE!" Pandemonium swept the room. Claws waved, fur bristled, eyes left their sockets and rolled up again. Furry feet stamped, crooked paws grabbed, fingernails shot in and out. Voices blew, bubbled, grated, shrieked, and wailed.

"We're not *leaving*! Ohhhhhhhh!" A great rasping breath sucked in the air of the room.

"Naaaaaahhhh!" A hideous, foul exhalation filled it.

"*Not leaving!*" came a chorus of improbable voices, and Frankie staggered toward the angel. "Oh, Mister, you got to be kidding!"

All of the shapes and shadows and fur and claws and fangs moved nearer to the angel. "We won't leave!" Wolf Demon's eyes burned bright red.

"That's an impossibility, my dear sir," Vampire whipped his black cape around him.

Bats, ravens, and vultures fanned their wings and blew their horrid breath in the angel's face. He trembled.

"Retreat, you miserable Horde!" he cried fearfully as they kept advancing. "Out!"

Growls, gurgles, disjointed shrieks, masses of fur and talons, and hot breath blew at him. The sleeves of his coat caught fire, and he tried to pat it out. Without wings, the angel felt helpless, terrified, he couldn't fly away.

"Oh, now, my dear friends," said the angel, "just because a little boy wants you to leave...."

A blob of green jelly slimed across the floor, grew tall, and towered over him. Tentacles appeared to reach out and slide toward his frail, white cord feet. Two pale green spots, like stalks of asparagus, grew out of a face and stared at him. A red mouth with black teeth appeared to smile, as it uttered, "Never go away, never go away...."

The improbable chorus echoed it, "We'll never go away, never go away...."

And the angel suddenly gave up. He trembled and retreated inside. In his dream, Peter could feel him giving up. Feel what it was like to be inside that barrel body with the corded arms and legs, the stiff, wicker head, the black wheel eyes—and no wings.

The angel started to laugh and laugh. He laughed until he drowned out all the Horde with his laughter. And finally he said, "It's okay, boys. I was only kidding. Don't you know I'm only a monster in disguise—just like you?"

And he grew ten feet tall. The barrel filled the room. He grew and swelled and rose on his white cord legs. His fingers and toes snaked out, his rubber wheel eyes blinked, the taped mouth opened and closed—as he stalked toward Peter's bunk.

11

Eliza wanted to leave the church they'd found and look for another. "We have to find a different sort of angel!"

But Eben was sure they'd done quite enough exploring for one night. "We were lucky to find a church at all, Eliza! It's cozy and warm in here. If you must look for another, we'll do it tomorrow."

"Tomorrow won't do, Mr. Starbuck. Peter needs help right now!"

"Why can't these angels lend a hand?" grumbled Eben. "I don't see anything the matter with 'em at all."

"They're just not *strong* enough, Eben." Eliza gazed up at the pictures. "They're very sweet and pretty and I'm sure they're good and loving angels too. I don't mean to be rude to them—but not one of them is Peter's angel."

"What makes you think you'd *know* Peter's angel if you saw it?" asked Eben.

"I don't know how I'll know, Mr. Starbuck, but I'll know."

Eben wriggled impatiently. "I wish I could see what you have in mind, Eliza."

"Oh, it's not in my mind—it's somewhere else entirely." Eliza began nosing along the floor.

"I doubt if we can get out anyway," Eben reminded her. "The doors are closed and locked."

But Eliza paid no attention. She scrabbled this way and that over the red carpet, and finally nosed out a draught of cold air on the floor. Reluctantly Eben followed, until she found a crack beneath one of the church doors. "Here's our way out, Mr. Starbuck!"

They squeezed under the door and out into the cold New York night. "There, that wasn't so bad, was it?"

"Except that my stomach is squashed, and it's freezing," said Eben.

"Then let's run to keep warm!"

They ran north up the avenue, past stores that were closed for the night. But Eliza wasn't content to run in one direction. She made excursions down every side street so they wouldn't miss a church along the way. Eben couldn't keep up with her. On her fourth side trip he was so exhausted that he waited on the corner, and when Eliza returned a few minutes later she was wet, bedraggled, dirty, dripping, and shivering all over.

"Oh, my word! What happened, Eliza?"

"I fell in the gutter!" she replied. "I didn't notice the curb — it was high — and there was water — dirty water — where I fell."

"Oh dear, oh dear, Mrs. Starbuck."

"It doesn't matter," she squeaked through chattering teeth. "You were wrong about New York, Eben! There must be hundreds of churches here — I found another! It's bigger and there may be bigger and stronger angels inside."

Eben took a moment to rub Eliza's wet back and then they ran down the street together. The church she had found was much larger than the last, with not one, but two towers on either side of a high-peaked roof. They found a way in beneath a small side door and crept past an enormous desk where a gray-haired lady was working late. Beyond the office was a small hallway filled with burning candles and then the inside of the church.

It was entirely different from the last. Here were dark wooden pews, rather than red plush seats, and everything smelled musty and old.

Eben and Eliza crept down a long aisle, until they reached the front row of pews. Ahead was a large white marble altar. And on either side, rising from high platforms, were two towering, massively winged, white marble angels.

"I knew they'd be big!" Eliza clasped her paws together.

"They're certainly large enough," breathed Eben.

The angels towered high above them, their heads tilted back as they blew brass trumpets into the sky. Their marble gowns blew in quiet, graceful folds around their feet. They looked enormous, majestic, and serene.

"They look too cold," said Eliza suddenly.

"They are made of *marble*, Mrs. Starbuck! If you were made of marble, you might look cold too."

"What they're made of, Eben, doesn't matter. It's what they are inside. Those angels are too content — they're not fighters."

"Of course they're not fighters, Mrs. Starbuck! They're blowers of trumpets! If you were a marble angel blowing trumpet, you'd be content too."

"Well," Eliza sighed, "they're very beautiful and certainly big enough — but neither one is Peter's angel!" She sneezed and started coughing.

Eben moved closer to warm her.

"We can't go on looking for angels forever, Eliza. You're catching cold. One of these angels must surely do." He looked around the church. "Why, there are hundreds of angels here. All around, as far as the eye can see."

Eliza craned her neck. "I can't see them very well, they're all too far away. But even from here they look much too quiet and peaceful."

"Isn't that what an angel means, Eliza—*peace?*" asked Eben with some frustration.

"Maybe...after a while," she said thoughtfully. "But driving away monsters isn't such a peaceful task."

"I don't know, Eliza," said Eben wearily. "They look like a regular army of angels to me."

"One angel of just the right sort," said Eliza firmly, "could do more than an entire army!"

Eliza looked up to the far ceiling and around the church at all the hundreds and hundreds of angels. From over her head and from all around they smiled down quietly, contentedly, peacefully.

"You won't do," said Eliza. "You won't do at all — and I have a feeling you know that. But since we're here and you're here and we're here all together—and there are so very, very many of you — would you try to do the best you can?

"I mean," she continued, "try to keep Peter safe for the night?"

84

12

Peter awoke feeling very peculiar. He was hot and cold and shivering all over. He put his hand to his forehead — no fever. He was still just terrified. The nightmare seemed to have gone on all night long. He was exhausted! And still so scared that he didn't want to get up. It took him a few minutes to remember it was Saturday and he didn't have to. He heard a high wind whistling and sleet rattling against his windowpanes. That scared him too. He groaned and pulled the covers way over his head.

The last time he'd had such a nightmare, the mice had been there to comfort him. Peter lifted one small corner of the blanket and sneaked a look at the mouse hole. His heart sank. The brownie

crumbs were just where he'd left them. Somehow he'd hoped his little friends might return. He didn't think he could work on the angel without their presence. He hardly knew what he was making any more, an angel or a monster.

He didn't dare look at the barrel! Peter shivered again and burrowed deep under his blankets. He might never get up again!

The doorbell rang.

It rang again — and again — and nobody went to answer. On Saturday mornings his parents slept late. Who could it possibly be? On Saturday mornings they used to have Monster Club meetings, but now....

Peter took a deep breath, leaped from his bunk with the blanket still covering his head, and ran to the front door.

He had never been so glad to see anyone in his life!

There were Obie and Sal together, and Sal was presenting something to him on a cloth-covered tray.

"Hi, Pete," she grinned. "I made a brain for your angel."

Peter had never thought of giving the angel a brain. And it sounded too much, he thought, like *The Wizard of Oz*. He looked at the tray as she set it down on his desk.

"Is that really an angel's brain?" he asked suspiciously.

"I think so. I *hope* so," said Sal quite honestly. "I did the best I could." She lifted a corner of the cloth and sighed. "Isn't it beautiful?"

Peter didn't think so. He examined the hard, cold, gray clay. "It looks awfully heavy to me."

Sal thought it was a little heavy for an angel's brain too, but she didn't want to say so. She'd worked for hours on it. Then, when she was all finished, she'd had a terrific inspiration about what an angel's brain really *should* be.

But all she said now was, "Don't put it in until

the last minute, Pete. If it gets jogged around too much it might break."

Obie was staring at the barrel-creature. "That's terrific, Pete. But does it look like an angel to you?"

With his friends there in the room, Peter found the courage to throw back his blanket and look.

And he jumped!

Sitting there in the raincoat and mop hair, it looked almost real. As if it could easily arise from the floor on those white cord legs and stalk around.

Obie said temptingly, "It would sure make a terrific monster, Pete."

He didn't have to be told! Peter shivered and looked over his shoulder. Was the Horde still around? He wondered how Obie would feel if he had to live with monsters all day, all night. He was even tempted to give the angel to Obie. Maybe the Horde would follow, and move up to Obie's house.

"Hoo, hoo!" came a few jeers, as Peter looked around. The eye of the Giant Green Slug in the picture slowly winked at him. So that's where they were this morning! Hiding in the pictures. Probably thinking they were cute and funny, teasing him.

Peter shuddered. Well, he certainly couldn't go

through another night like last night. It would *have* to be an angel!

"Maybe it doesn't look like one because it doesn't have wings yet," said Peter.

"Can we help you make the wings?" asked Obie eagerly.

"I thought you didn't like angels."

"Well, but this one ... this one's kind of different." (It looked even more like a monster than Obie had expected, and he was delighted.) "What are you going to use for wings?"

"They should be feathery and sweeping," mused Peter. "If we collected a lot of feathers we could glue them onto a frame."

"But feathers wouldn't be strong enough," Sal objected. "You want it to fly, don't you?"

Peter remembered his nightmare and the angel helpless, without wings. "I sure want it to be *able* to fly!"

Obie and Sal sent secret smiles to each other and Obie suggested temptingly, "If we took it up to the roof when there's lightning, Pete, maybe we could sort of ...bring it to life."

"And it might really fly!" urged Sal.

Visions of Dr. Frankenstein's laboratory flashed through Peter's mind. Visions of electrical equipment and lightning striking Frankie's body. Would it work for an angel too? A delicious chill ran through him.

"We ... we wouldn't have any electricity," he whispered' "for a hook-up."

"I don't think you'd need it to bring an angel to life," said Sal seriously. "Just nature ought to do."

"But where would it fly?" wondered Peter.

"Up over the roof!" said Obie.

"I don't want it to fly away!" cried Peter. Even with wings, he'd visualized the angel constantly on vigil in his room.

"Oh, he'd come back — wouldn't he? After all, he's your angel," said Sal.

The picture was thrilling. His angel, soaring over the roof, high over Manhattan in the winter sky — that'd show the monsters a thing or two!

"There's going to be a storm tonight," prompted Obie. "I heard it on the weather report. Thunder and lightning and a big wind."

"But what could we use for wings?" frowned Peter.

"Would kites be strong enough?" asked Obie.

"I don't think so, they're just paper. Maybe we should get some strong cloth and sew that over a frame."

"But that would take days," Obie complained.

Sal clapped her hands. "An umbrella!"

"Yes!" said Peter. "If we cut an umbrella in half it really would look like two wings."

"But then the wind wouldn't lift it," said Obie.

"Two umbrellas!" said Peter.

"Two umbrellas might bump into each other," said Obie.

"Not if they were the right size," cried Sal. "Like those small round ones — like mine."

They all became excited. Sal's umbrella was just the right size and made of transparent plastic. Peter thought it would look quite like an angel's wing.

"But they have to match," he said. "Where can we get another one?"

"A friend of mine has one," offered Sal. "Maybe she'd let us borrow it."

"Where is she?"

"A couple of blocks. Come on, Obie," said Sal, who liked company in whatever she did.

When they left, Peter went to his window. Sleet was driving in sheets across the river and the wind whistled eerily. A fine storm was blowing up. "Tonight," dreamed Peter, "tonight on the roof."

After the wings were attached there was one last thing to do. Peter had known from the first that a halo was what made an angel an angel. He would put it on last, and then, if lightning really struck it....

"Sure you know what you're doing, kid?" Frankie's voice rumbled from the wall.

Peter turned. Hiding in the pictures was somehow worse than when they were "out."

"Don't tell him!" slurped the Giant Slug.

"What the kid don't know won't hurt him," said Wolf Demon.

They were only trying to scare him, thought Peter, hoping that the angel would be a monster. "And I'll bet," he thought to himself, "that Obie and Sal hope so too." He looked at Sal's brain, wondering if he should use it. If he didn't, it would hurt her feelings.

He walked to his closet to get the halo. It was a circular television antenna that he'd kept for years, not knowing why, or what he would ever use it for. He held it in his hand, thinking that he would have to attach a straight wire on the back, making it high enough to encircle the angel's head.

"For your information, kid," said Frankie, "bad angels have halos too."

"Shut up!" called the others.

But Frankie went on. "A nice monster is a much better thing to have around the house than a bad angel. Think about that, kid."

Peter stared at the poster. And from his prone position on Dr. Frankenstein's laboratory couch, Frankie winked back.

13

Of course, Eben and Eliza had no idea that Peter had misunderstood their "message" of the plugged-up door. They never dreamed he thought they had "abandoned" him. When they woke up in church that morning Eliza couldn't wait to get started again.

"It's hard to turn our days and nights upside down like this," complained Eben as they crawled out from the pages of the Bible where they'd spent the night. The bible was in a rack behind a pew, and there they had slept to keep warm.

Eliza's response was a sneeze. Her cold was worse and Eben was sniffling as well. They jumped to the floor and felt icy draughts creeping through the church.

"The weather has changed," said Eben.

"Yes, it's much colder than it was last night."

But neither of them was prepared for the weather that met them outdoors. They hid behind a corner near the church doors, waiting for someone to open them. When the janitor came by to unlock they were ready to dart out. They skittered and slid and tumbled over and over down the steps outside that were covered with a film of ice. At the bottom they were pelted with particles of the sleet Peter had heard on his windows.

"This is awful!" cried Eben, trying to run over the slippery, icy sidewalk.

"T-terrible," agreed Eliza, sliding around.

"We'll have to get in somewhere, Eliza!"

But they could find no cozy hole, no warm basement to get out of the terrible weather. At the corner they had no choice but to put their backs to the wind. It blew them north, past a photograph store, a bridal shop, a funeral parlor, an auto parts store — nothing was open this early.

In front of the auto parts store was a stack of rubber tires, held sideways in a rack, on display. They jumped up inside, only to find it cold and icy, with a pile of slush at one end.

"At least we're out of the wind for a moment," said Eben, looking around the black rubber walls.

"And we needn't be thirsty," said Eliza, lapping

at the slush which was cleaner than that on the street.

"We'll have to find something to eat," said Eben. He looked out the end of the tires and surveyed the sidewalk. Next to the street was a straggly, stunted tree on a plot of littered earth. Mixed with the slush were gum wrappers, bottles, a can, and— Eben spotted something.

He jumped down and came back a minute later dragging the end of an old hot dog. "Both bun and meat," he said proudly. The bun was half hard and half soggy, and the frankfurter piece was icy cold. But they ate gratefully while around them the slick rubber got colder and damper by the minute.

"Let's go on," said Eliza, "before we freeze to death right here!"

They jumped out, and still the wind pushed them north. It pressed down on their tails and then nearly lifted them across another street. Still there was no open basement, no friendly light, only a huge, gray building that took up the whole block.

"It's dangerous here," cried Eben. "There's no place to hide."

But Eliza had seen the outline of a telephone booth. "At the corner," she pointed. They slipped over the sidewalk and stopped by the side of the booth. Across the street they could see the outlines of trees and a building with pointed spires.

"It may be a church!" cried Eliza.

"I don't care what it is," said Eben, "as long as we can get in somewhere."

The curb was high and the gutter was filled with ice and dirt, but they found a place to leap over and skidded across the street. As they climbed up on the opposite curb the hail began to lessen—and yet the wind pushed them on.

Eliza looked for the building with spires, feeling they'd gone beyond it. Every inch of her tiny body was trembling and she didn't know how much longer she could run. As she looked up and around, the sky began to clear, and Eliza suddenly stopped to cry, "Eben!"

The sun had broken through the dark clouds over the city, and the wind was blowing them away. They moved swiftly to the north, leaving wide, broken patches of blue. And straight up ahead, in a wide, clear window in the sky, rose the walls of the largest, mightiest building she had ever seen.

She squinted in the sudden sunlight. Way up on the roof, and far away, she saw the figure of a tall and glorious angel blowing a trumpet into the sky. And he didn't seem at all like the trumpeting angels of the other church—he didn't seem cold—

he looked warm in the light of the sun, and glowing, and he almost seemed to be in motion. As if, with his trumpet, he was calling the whole, wide world.

"Oh, Eben," cried Eliza, "I think we've found the Cathedral!"

14

When Eben and Eliza reached the top of the
Cathedral steps they couldn't find a way inside.
The huge central bronze doors were tightly sealed
and there wasn't a hint of a crack to squeeze
through. They found another entry, but it looked
very tricky and dangerous. It was a set of double
glass doors with an open area between them—and
no place to hide.

"Not even a shadow!" said Eben, "If we got
caught in the middle."

"But we have to try, Eben." Eliza peeked in the
first glass door. "We'll have to scoot in when
someone else goes in — or out."

"Eliza!" Eben warned her. "We're bound to be seen. Those doors look like a regular trap to me. Let's just wait and see how they work."

They huddled in a shadow against the icy wall, shivering and uncertain. Just then a young Father with a pleasant face came out from the Cathedral, through the glass doors, and his long habit brushed right past them.

"There's our answer, Eben!" squeaked Eliza with delight. "When he goes back, run under his skirts!"

"Skirts!" Eben stared at the heavy habit. Underneath were big black shoes, and they looked awfully powerful. "We'll get kicked! And that skirt isn't long enough to hide us."

"Yes, it is—and there's a shadow where it falls. We can do it if we're fast enough. Get ready, Eben, it's the only way!"

The Father had walked to the head of the steps and was looking up at the clearing sky. He walked a little to the north and south, breathing in the morning. He turned with a smile to look up at the Cathedral towers and then strode back to the door.

When he put his hand on the brass pull, Eben and Eliza ducked in under his habit, right beside his feet. He pulled the first door open, crossed the dangerous area with two large steps, and opened the second door. The mice had to hurry to keep up with his flying feet—and the swinging skirt and shadows blocked their view. All they could see were the heavy shoes beside them.

When suddenly the Father stopped abruptly, they kept right on running. It took them a moment to realize they were no longer under the sheltering skirts.

Eben and Eliza squeaked! And ducked swiftly under a row of seats.

The Father stood bemused for a moment, listening, blinking, and rubbing his eyes. Then he smiled, shook his head, and walked away. His footsteps echoed loudly, then quietly, and then became fainter and fainter. Eben and Eliza waited with pounding hearts until he'd gone.

Then, very cautiously and quietly, they crept under a long row of seats until they came to a wide central aisle. They stopped by the last chair to look out, and up, and around. They had come about a quarter of the way down the length of the immense Cathedral.

And they were in a whole new world, Eben felt, with a ground, and distance, and a sky all its own. The vast, vaulted ceiling arched miles above their heads. Shafts of light shone through high, stained-glass windows, spilling out colors of red and blue and gold and green and violet. All around was marble and gleaming wood.

It was like being someplace even bigger than outdoors, thought Eben, and he trembled — he was so small. The other churches hadn't been like this — even the streets of New York hadn't been like this! Feeling dismayed and utterly insignificant, he curled up in a tiny mouse outline under the seat.

Eliza's nose was out to the vaulted ceiling. "Where are the angels?" her whiskers twitched.

Her small squeak echoed in the awesome silence. Even Eliza, with an angel quest to sustain her, felt a twinge of fear. The great Cathedral was not like anything she had ever imagined. Not even in her dreams when sometimes, instead of dreaming of the Nantucket attic, she would have strange dreams of the deep blue sky and the stars.

She coughed, and the sound reverberated up to the ceiling and down again. "Shh," Eben clapped a paw against her mouth.

From somewhere they heard indistinct voices and the tread of feet. Eliza was trying to sense a direction. There must be hundreds of angels here, but everything was so far away. Where would she find Peter's angel? He must be here — an angel large and strong enough, in a space small enough for her to find. Perhaps somewhere in the direction of that angel on the roof?

102

"Come, Eben." Eliza started off where instinct led her, back to the north aisle, and then east. She headed straight for the high altar and the circle of chapels that surrounded it in the rear.

Hugging the side walls they crossed an open area and saw a flight of steps. Eben wanted to turn left, but Eliza said, "No, straight on."

Footsteps echoed behind them and sudden fear made them run. Eliza flashed up the steps, through the gate, turned and disappeared. Eben lost her in the deep shadows of the aisle behind the high altar. He crept along slowly, searching. Then, with a squeak of recognition, he turned and pattered softly into one of the seven chapels.

He had seen Peter's Angel too. And now he knew what Eliza had meant when she said, "I don't know how I'll know, but I'll know." For there was no doubt about it — this was the angel they'd been seeking.

Eliza crouched on the floor, still as a statue herself, before the immense bronze figure. He stood against the wall of the small chapel dressed in armor and a shirt of mail. A visor was thrown back over his helmeted head. His strong right hand gripped an enormous sword. And from his shoulders rose the mightiest wings in the world. They curved far above his head, sweeping, powerful, ready in an instant to fly away.

The Archangel Michael looked out over the chapel with a serene yet watchful expression. In back of those deep eyes there seemed to be a memory of many ancient battlegrounds.

Eliza clasped her paws together. Her eyes were moist. But quickly she was brisk and businesslike. There was work to do.

"We've been looking for you," she began.

Behind them came a sudden roar of sound. It broke like a tidal wave, flooding the small chapel. The vibration rose through Eben's feet and shook his body; his bones seemed to melt in a sea of sound. Someone was playing the great organ. With a deep shudder, Eben put his paws over his ears and squeezed shut his eyes.

When he opened them again, Eliza had jumped up to one of the rush seats nearer the Angel. Light was streaming through the stained-glass windows and glinting off his huge sword. Eben followed Eliza as she jumped off the seat to the base of the statue. There, between the Angel's feet, they looked up into the strong, shining face.

And it seemed to both of them, through the roar of bone-shattering sound, that the Archangel Michael was slowly moving his head.

15

Peter held the television antenna over the angel's head, wondering how it would finally look when he attached it.

"Not right," said Peter at last. "It just looks like a circle of wire."

He walked back a few paces. In a sense his creation was perfect. It belonged in his room along with masks, models, bugs, and monster pictures. But it didn't belong as an angel.

"Could it be the room that's wrong?" wondered Peter. He contemplated his horror collection. "Maybe it isn't the proper environment? Sister's always talking about the environment," he went on to the angel. "Water, air, cities, the things we live in the middle of, you know. Maybe you can't live in the middle of all this?"

The tape mouth was silent, the rubber eyes stared at him blankly.

"Maybe it's impossible to make an angel in a room like this?"

Come to think of it, Peter had never seen an angel in such a room. The only angels he had seen lived in churches, chapels, cathedrals.

"I can't turn my room into a church!" he cried helplessly. "That's not what you want, is it?

He considered. "But I guess I could get rid of... of all this. I was going to eventually, anyway."

But Peter was afraid to do it alone. He had hoped Obie and Sal would take down the collection. "I could wait until they come back with your wings."

The angel remained quietly on the floor, looking slightly forlorn. Come to think of it, Peter had never seen an angel sitting on the floor like that. "Perhaps you'd be more comfortable in a chair?" he suggested politely.

He lifted the barrel body to his seat at the desk and turned the chair so the angel faced the room. His back sat up quite straight and the cord legs dangled down neatly. "That's better! Now you can watch," said Peter.

"I guess there are some things in this world you

have to do all alone," he sighed. And scared as he was, Peter felt the angel had to see him do it.

It wouldn't even be fair to the monsters, he reflected, to wait for Obie and Sal. The Horde had been his special friends for over a year now, and removing them gave Peter a funny feeling. It was almost like having to shoot your own horse — a little different, of course.

"You see," he told the angel, frowning, "I know very well who I want you to be, but I don't know who you really are. Maybe if you don't have all this ... stuff ... to distract you, *you* can figure it out. I guess it's up to you now, but this is the least I can do for you."

He began by pulling the bugs down from the ceiling. Forty jumps, forty fast pulls, and he had them all. He removed the skeletons from the window shades and the Halloween masks from the door. He piled all his make-up, monster models, magazines, and horror comics in a huge stack on his bunk. He emptied a carton of toys from his closet and swept everything inside the box.

Then, nervously, Peter approached a poster. For the first, he deliberately chose one of his lesser monsters, the Great Scaled Moth, who didn't show up very often. Nevertheless, Peter expected it to materialize at any moment, and fly at him with its huge scaly wings.

At the very least he expected his old, familiar, day-to-day Horde to jump out and complain! His hands were sweating. Peter looked at the posters of Frankie, Wolf Demon, the Blob; he gazed at the chewed picture of Dracula. If little mice could be that brave....

Quickly, Peter ripped the Great Scaled Moth from the wall. Nothing happened. He took down Wolf Demon. Silence. He removed the Blob, the Slime, the Mud Men twins — and another — and another. Still nothing. No voices or eyes winking and blinking at him. But when he came to Frankie, Peter paused. It gave him a terrible feeling.

"Sorry," he said swiftly, "but it's got to be done!" He gave a great, shuddering sigh, and took down Frankie.

Peter removed his entire collection of pictures, placed them all on top of the box, and carried it out to the hall, to leave for Obie and Sal.

When he came back to his room it looked as barren and empty as if he'd just moved in. With the monsters gone there seemed to be nothing left of Peter, nothing to say he'd ever lived there. Only some old string dangling from the ceiling, and pieces of old scotch tape on the walls.

And that mop-haired, barrel-chested, rain-coated figure sitting at his desk, looking somehow like a guest who'd just arrived. It seemed to be waiting for something. In the empty room, Peter noticed that the mop hair was filled with dust balls and the basket face was streaked with dirt.

"Oh! Maybe you need to get washed," said Peter. "Aren't angels supposed to be clean?"

He pulled out the dust from the hair, got a wet washrag and soap from his bathroom, and rubbed the angel's face. For good measure he gave a swipe at the fingers and toes. He peeked under the raincoat and saw the barrel was dusty all over. The wires he'd used stuck out in crooked points and snarls. He lifted the lid of the basket. There was loads of dust inside the angel's head. And tangles of old thread, and a safety pin stuck in the wicker.

"Maybe that's what's wrong," said Peter. "An angel should be as perfect on the inside as the outside — I think."

He took off the raincoat and started all over again, dusting and cleaning and washing. He straightened out the wires as neatly as he could. But when he was finished the angel didn't look that different.

"You're still sort of freakish," said Peter. "But there's one more thing to do."

This was the part he'd been waiting for all along. He went out through the kitchen to the back hall and got a large stack of old newspapers. He went back to the pantry and opened the paint cupboard. He took a jar, a brush, a stick, a tin of turpentine, and the can of gold paint his mother sometimes used for antiquing furniture. He shook the can and listened. If there wasn't enough, he'd have to go out for more. He couldn't tell by shaking, so he pried off the lid with a can opener. Plenty! It was three quarters full.

Peter took everything back to his room and opened the windows wide. Cold air blew in, rattling the newspapers as he laid them on the floor, on the desk, and under the angel's chair.

"This ought to do it," he smiled, stirring up the paint. First he painted the halo straight from the can, and set it aside to dry. Then he made a thinner mixture of paint and turpentine in the jar. It had to be thin, to dry by tonight. He painted the barrel, inside and out, and the basket head. He painted the whole face, nose, eyes and mouth.

He tried to paint each strand of the mop but it was too hard. So Peter emptied the jar over the angel's hair. Gold rivers ran down the wire neck, the cord arms, and made a puddle on the newspaper below. Peter used the drips to paint all the fingers and toes.

He laid the raincoat on the floor and began to paint that too. But instantly he saw it wouldn't work. The material refused to take the paint; it just smeared and looked horribly messy.

"Oh, no!" cried Peter. "What'll I do? You've got to be dressed in gold!" He had counted on painting the coat.

His mind ran over everything in the apartment. Was there anything — clothes, drapes, towels, bedspreads — he could use? Anything stuffed away?

"Christmas paper!" He suddenly thought of the hall closet where his mother saved wrapping paper. He had a memory of something gold and sparkling from last year.

He ran out, shoved all the coats in the closet to one end, and found the crumpled shopping bag shoved back in one corner. Tall rolls of paper stuck out from the top, red, green, blue—and yes —*gold!*

He grabbed the whole bag, got his father's heavy duty stapler, and went back to his room. He rolled out the gold paper on the floor. Was there enough? Not really—but there were other stray gold pieces folded in the bottom of the bag. He started cutting. He cut long strips from the roll and stapled them on the front and back of the coat. He cut shorter, horizontal strips, and stapled them around the sleeves. He patched the pockets and collar with smaller pieces from the bottom of the shopping bag.

He'd forgotten the belt! And he was almost out

of paper. He dumped out the entire contents of the bag. From the very bottom, underneath the paper, out fell colored Christmas ribbons, and shiny red and gold bows.

"Ahhh!" sighed Peter with relief. He worked out all the gold bows and stapled them straight across the belt.

He began to have a delicious feeling in his stomach. The coat looked even better this way. It sparkled and glittered in many different golden shades. He stood up to look at the angel and noticed the brain still sitting on his desk.

Sal! She'd be so disappointed. Peter didn't know about that brain, but he took the last of the mixture from the jar and gave it a few swipes—just in case.

Then he stood back, brush in hand, to look at the sparkling coat and the angel. As the paint began to dry, he was glittering and sparkling too.

"This is it!" said Peter excitedly. "There he is! My wonderful, tough, golden angel!"

"Don't be too sure," someone growled.

Peter froze. Slowly he looked away from the angel, and his stomach turned over. In every place where he'd removed a picture, the monsters were back again! They'd gone to black and white instead of color, but they pressed against the walls in their old, familiar places, winking and blinking, and talking at him.

"Didn't think you could get rid of us that easily?" howled Wolf Demon.

"This is our home, kid. You don't kick people out of their homes just like that," complained Frankie.

"Yeah, a landlord's got to give notice," the Vampire grinned.

"It's a law, kid," Frankie reminded him.

"You'll have to take it to court," said the Blob and the Slime.

And the Mud Men giggled, "Haw, haw, take it to court, to court, to court...."

Vast shouts and hoots and howls of outrage and mirth drowned the room. Peter put his gold spattered hands over his ears to close out the sound. The monsters were still jeering and hooting and teasing when Obie and Sal came back in.

16

It was nighttime and Peter's angel rode up in the elevator. His golden eyes stared straight ahead, his golden mouth was smiling. His golden fingers swayed, side to side, and his golden toes seemed to dance. The angel looked happier now with his two transparent umbrella wings.

Peter and Obie and Sal had cut slits in the back of the coat, to hook them over the barrel hoop. Then they'd secured them with wire. The wings were folded down now, but they shone with reflected light from his glittering coat and his long, golden hair.

"He's beautiful!" breathed Sal. "He almost looks like an angel. Don't you think so, Obie?"

"I guess so." Obie, who was holding the angel up on one side, looked away uncomfortably. He didn't know if he could pretend it was a monster anymore. It looked far too much like an angel to suit him. It was a sissy spectacle and Obie didn't want to be seen with him. "I hope nobody else is going up," he muttered.

"Yes," said Peter, who was holding the other side, "I don't want anybody to see him. If we stop, stand in front of him, Sal."

"I will, but you should want the whole world to see him!" Sal was carrying the brain, and had the halo looped over her coat sleeve. They were all wrapped to their ears in coats, hats, and scarfs, against the weather.

"Fourteen, fifteen," counted Peter as they rose, "sixteen, seventeen. Good! We're here."

Sal held the door while Obie and Peter struggled out with the angel. Seventeen was the top floor but they still had to carry it up a flight of steps to the roof. Sal went up first and stopped at the landing. "We should put in the brain and put the halo on here," she said. "It'll be too windy outside."

Carefully, Peter and Obie sat the angel on the top step and propped him, with his umbrella wings, against the side walls.

Sal began to giggle. "If you left him here and the superintendent came up, what do you suppose he'd think? That the building has a guardian angel?"

Peter couldn't even smile. He was grimly watching the steps below. At any moment he expected the Horde to appear. Obie and Sal weren't aware of it, but when they'd all taken the angel from Peter's room, the Horde had quietly stepped down from the walls. Like tall, strangely flattened, black and white shadows, they had followed the children out to the hall. At the elevator, as usual, they had disappeared. Peter didn't like their absence one bit. He felt they had some awful surprise in store.

Sal, holding the brain, looked thoughtfully at the angel. He'd come out so much better than she'd ever expected. He was almost pretty. No— he was strange. Golden and strange and ... interesting. She liked him. No— she loved him.

"Well, go on, go on," urged Obie. "Put in the brain, Sal."

Peter looked up from the stairs. He was about to say he wasn't at all sure about that brain, but he didn't have to. Because Sal suddenly dropped it. It slid off the plate and smashed on the cement landing into a thousand little pieces of gold flecked gray clay.

With a strange little smile Sal said, "Oh, dear!"

Obie said, "Oh, too bad, Sal!"

But Sal looked at Peter and grinned. She wasn't at all sorry. In fact, she felt so much better that she thought the moment called for honesty.

"I wasn't sure about that brain anyway. It was too heavy and I don't know much about angels. I ...I thought," said Sal, "that maybe they have light and airy thoughts, and this might be even better."

She dug into her coat pocket and whipped out a golden balloon.

"A balloon brain," cried Peter, "oh, no!"

"But it's *light*," said Sal, "and it might even help him to fly."

Peter looked at the balloon. He looked at Sal whose mouth was beginning to work strangely. She was even swallowing in a most disturbing way.

Something overcame Peter. She had cared enough to really think about it, she had *tried*....

"Okay, Sal," he smiled. "Let's blow it up. I think that's a great idea!"

She grinned and started puffing. When she lost her breath Peter took over. Together they finally had a nice fat, airy balloon which fit neatly into the basket head.

And then Sal held out the halo to Peter. "You should put this on," she smiled, "because it's the very last thing."

Obie looked away, embarrassed. This entire procedure was becoming far too serious and important to suit him. It was the sissiest thing he'd ever been involved in and even Sal was involved! He kicked the smashed pieces of the clay brain away with his foot, thinking, "There goes a great monster."

Peter wasn't thinking at all. He was far too nervous, waiting for the Horde to appear. He took the halo and hooked the tall piece of wire to the back of the angel's neck. It floated above, golden, encircling, quite lovely.

"Come on, come on," urged Obie, anxious for the adventure to end. "Let's get it out to the roof."

"Hang on tight when Sal opens the door," cautioned Peter. "He might blow away."

"He can't blow away," scoffed Obie. "You put on too much paint."

But when Sal opened the roof door they had to clutch the angel tightly. Wind whipped and tore and grabbed at them. Holding the angel between them, Peter and Obie were carried a few feet forward, and then pushed back. The force of the wind took their breaths away. Finally they backed up into the side of a water tower.

Sal managed to close the door, and then skidded across the roof, leaning backward in the wind. "This is great!" she yelled, "but where's the lightning?"

The sky was lit with a peculiar yellow-purple glow. The moon sailed in and out between masses of heavy gray cloud. All around them dark roof-tops reached away over the city. The wind was shrieking and blowing north — northeast. Peter and Obie tried to steady the angel against the side of the water tower, but it leaped and strained under their hands. The gold paper on the coat started to tear and crackle.

"When we open the umbrellas," shouted Obie, excited again, "I think it really will fly!"

Peter grabbed at the angel's arm. Now they were here, he didn't want it to fly! It was beautiful. It *did* look like an angel. Maybe it *was* an angel! He wanted it right where he'd always seen it in the first place. In his room, sitting in a corner, guarding and protecting him.

A tremendous clap of thunder smashed to the west. Lightning illuminated the river. Sal ran over the roof, flapping her arms in the wind. "Quick, quick, before the wind dies down!"

Obie started to open an umbrella.

"Stop!" shouted Peter. "I don't want him to fly!"

But Sal was helping too, and both umbrellas popped open. As Peter tried to stop them, a gust of wind pulled the angel out of their hands. It pushed against the umbrellas, dragging him across the roof. His gold legs scraped over the tar. He banged into the low wall at the edge, and stopped.

Peter ran after Obie and Sal who were trying to

catch him. But they were already there, and lifting him up — and with a little thrust, wind filled the umbrellas. The angel soared up for a minute, and then went down, disappearing below the roof.

Peter got to the edge and leaned there, looking down. The angel was dropping fast. He was falling, down, down. They could see the top of the halo, trembling in the wind, and the gold hair streaming up. Pieces of gold paper ripped and tore in streamers. And then he was sailing up again, across the street, several stories below. He almost crashed into the opposite building, but the wind lifted him again. He rose, soaring high. He cleared the roof and was suddenly hanging out and above them, halfway across the street.

Thunder rolled above, almost over their heads. The angel was suddenly illuminated by a tremendous flash of lightning. It seemed to pierce through the transparent wings and strike the golden halo over his head.

He was transformed!

To Peter, he seemed to become a vast, helmeted, armored figure that filled the sky. His mighty wings beat the air around him; he turned his visored head watchfully, while his enormous sword swept through the night.

And winging toward him came more monsters

120

than Peter had ever dreamed existed. They came from all directions, and from above and below, to fill and surround the space around that great, golden angel.

There were Manticores and Yales, Vipers, Syrens, Dragons. There were mythological beasts with shining tails, curved horns, cloven hooves. There were medieval demons with men's faces, stag's haunches, red eyes, and shrill voices. They howled and screamed and beat their wings and flicked their strange, stinging tails.

The Horde was suddenly all around Peter and voices shouted in his ears.

"They are *real* monsters."

"Would you rather have them than us?"

"We are puny, paper-thin, compared to them."

"We've been invented."

"They are real!"

"We're not so bad!"

"We've been a help."

"You may not know it."

And they called to the great Angel, "It's unfair!"

"*We* helped him think of you!"

"He wouldn't have *thought* of you, if we hadn't pestered him!"

"Unfair, unfair!"

"If he won't have us he shouldn't have anything at all!"

The angel's gleaming sword rose and sliced through the air. Beasts and demons tumbled, falling in all directions. The angel rose, beating his wings. And in the funnel of rushing air, the Horde behind Peter sailed up. They *were* paper-thin, like a rustle of newsprint in the sky. They streaked over his head, like shadowy, black-and-white cut-outs, and slantwise, fell toward the angel. They were entangled in a mass of flying, falling, struggling shapes, as the angel continued to rise and rise, his face intent, his sword sweeping, clearing a space, as his great wings made a wind in heaven.

A shudder ran through Peter. He was only nine and a half, so he closed his eyes.

When he opened them again, Obie and Sal were beside him, clutching his arms. And they were staring open-mouthed and goggle-eyed. "Look! Look at your angel!"

The umbrellas were raising him over the roofs. His gold fingers moved in the wind. Gold streamers flapped from his coat, and the sleeves of his outstretched arms. The wind was pushing him up and back and on, until he was sailing away.

The last Peter saw of his angel were his golden toes, streaming out in the night, as he flew north, over the roofs of Manhattan.

17

Eliza was dreaming one of her strange dreams about the deep blue sky and the stars.

But in this dream she wasn't alone — Eben was right beside her. They were soaring through the night sky, enclosed and protected by immense folding arms, against the rush of wind and cloud and stars. The stars sped by — or they seemed to speed by the stars.

From her secure place in the crook of the enormous arm, Eliza dreamed she looked down to see the world flow by beneath. Cities and highways flashed by, like medallions of jewels and long, silvery ribbons. There were patterns in the light and the dark, between shaded woods and dark

hills, and the sinewy loops of rivers—then curves and identations, and the moon gleaming on lacy surf that beat against a coastline. It was no longer night, the sun was rising. A warm, rosy glow spread over the waves as the sky turned first pink, then violet, then red.

Eliza dreamed she smelled salt in the air, then mist in the dawn, then a scent of wild rose and honeysuckle. And it wasn't November at all, but June, and they were soaring over Nantucket.

Above them the mighty wings flew steadily on and on, following the line of hills and pines and ponds and rolling moors, and then lower and lower over the trees and heath and marsh, until suddenly there was the old house by the sea with the shingled roof, and the welcoming attic, and the dear smell of old, familiar wood.

"Mmm!" Eliza stirred and murmured in her sleep. "I'm having the most wonderful dream, Mr. Starbuck!"

"I am too."

"Do you think we're dreaming the same dream, maybe?"

"Wouldn't be surprised."

"I'm dreaming of *home*, Eben."

"So'm I."

They pressed closer together.

"Wasn't it a glorious adventure, Eben?"

"Yes, it was. It still *is*, my dear Mrs. Starbuck."

"And we did find the right angel for Peter?"

"He couldn't have been better!" Eben sighed.

They fell asleep again, forgetting the cold in the Cathedral as they dreamed of the angel, and of Peter, and of going home.

18

"The Horde was right," thought Peter as he walked up Broadway the next day. "If it weren't for them I wouldn't have thought of an angel."

How could you think of an angel, he reflected, without a few monsters around to remind you? He supposed he ought to have thanked them. It was eerie to walk up the street with nobody following him. No hoots, or jeers, or sudden surprising catcalls.

He looked over his shoulder. No, there was no one there. Peter felt empty and strange, so alone, so "new," that he almost missed the Horde. "Thanks anyway," he said to the absent monsters. "It's too bad you didn't know how to keep your place. But there were too many of you; you were just too much."

And now he didn't even have his angel.

Obie and Sal wanted to go off on an expedition to find him, but Peter thought it was hopeless. The angel had probably crashed somewhere in a million gold-flecked pieces. He might be scattered over the city, smashed on a roof, even floating down the river. Maybe some little kid would find him sitting in a back yard.

Peter paused for the light at 110th Street. It was noon on Sunday and the sun was shining. The florists were open and beginning to display their Christmas decorations. Peter wished he could have kept the angel for Christmas. He would have liked to have had it in the corner.

He crossed the street, walked up two more blocks, and turned right to the Cathedral. He hadn't been there since that long-ago day when he and Obie had used it for horror chills. But Peter had awakened this morning with a memory that gave him a most peculiar feeling. He had to see for himself.

Before him rose the massive facade of the Cathedral. Peter ran up the steps and went in through the double glass doors. Inside, the feeling of space and weight immediately began to affect him. He felt strange, almost as haunted and shivery as that day with Obie. He tiptoed slowly up the aisle, past the bays and altars, and up the steps that led to the chapels behind the high altar. Then he

130

stopped outside the one he remembered and looked in.

Oh, yes! That was it! The same angel that had terrified them so on that long-ago day. The most "alive" statue in the whole Cathedral, at any moment about to turn its massive, helmeted head.

And the same angel of his "vision" on the roof last night!

What could it be but a vision? Later Peter had thought it was a trick of the light. A peculiar mixture of lightning, wind, and storm. Still, he couldn't get rid of the feeling that he'd seen a real angel — that his barrel had been transformed.

He lingered outside the chapel, gazing in at the tall, bronze figure with the immense wings and the mighty sword. "Tough," thought Peter. "Tough enough to handle anything."

He was so intent on looking that he didn't hear footsteps coming toward him. "It's the Archangel Michael," said a voice.

Peter almost jumped a mile.

"Oh! Sorry to startle you," said a young Father with a pleasant smile. "Did I see you at service this morning?"

"No," swallowed Peter, his heart still pounding. "I just came to see...him."

"Yes, lots of people are attracted by him." The Father was interested in a little boy who came to see an angel, so he confided, "You'd never guess who came to see him yesterday." He walked into the chapel and beckoned to Peter. "Come in. He's big, but you shouldn't be frightened."

Peter walked in and looked up at the angel's face. The same face. The deep eyes. The serious expression. That great sword.

" Guess who came to see him," said the Father. "You'll never guess. It was two mice. Two tiny gray mice."

"Mice?" asked Peter, bewildered.

"I found them right at his feet, on that cold, bronze base," said the Father. Seeing that Peter was afraid of the angel, he wanted him to touch it. "See what it's like. Feel."

Peter put his warm hand against the pounded bronze next to the angel's feet. It felt like ice, moving up to freeze the palm of his hand.

"I can't understand why they didn't rest on one of these." The Father pointed to kneeling cushions that lay in racks underneath the rush seats. "They would have been warm down there. Or they could have chosen one of our rugs, or a place closer to the heaters. But here they were."

He patted the base of the statue, and then ran his hand along the side of the angel's great wings. "Maybe they liked him," said the Father softly, "for some reason."

He looked down at Peter. "Would you like to see some other angels? We have lots of them in the